D0297624

THE
SISKIYOU
TWO-STEP

By the same author

DECOYS
30 FOR A HARRY
THE MANNA ENZYME
TROTSKY'S RUN

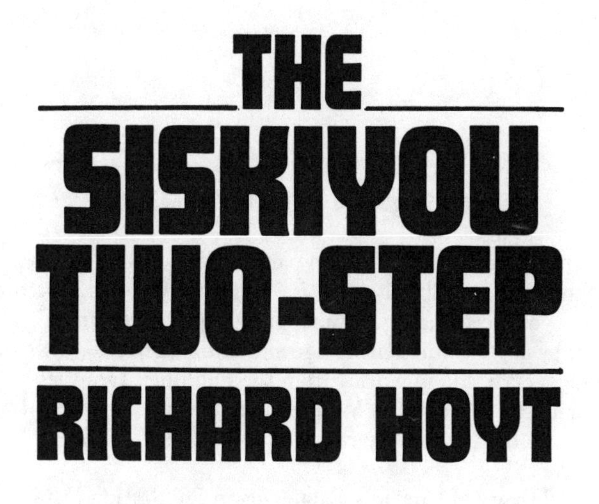

William Morrow and Company, Inc.
New York 1983

Library of Congress Cataloging in Publication Data

Hoyt, Richard, 1941-
The siskiyou two-step.

I. Title.
PS3558.O975S5 1983 813'.54 83-947
ISBN 0-688-01636-7

Printed in the United States of America

First Edition

1 2 3 4 5 6 7 8 9 10

BOOK DESIGN BY LINEY LI

This book is for my daughter, Laura.

Why, sir, of course I dance
As do we all from womb delivered;
The Lady watches whilst we prance:
One step this way, one step that.

—From *Jonathan Claiborne*
(The Sayani Manuscript)
by William Shakespeare

CHAPTER 1

I wish Zane Grey had been there. Maybe he would have known what to make of it all.

We were fishing at Steamboat on the North Umpqua River. Steamboat is one of the most famous steelhead drifts in the West. Zane Grey fished at Steamboat. Every summer fishermen gather there with their chest waders and ease out from the south shore to try their luck.

It is there, at Steamboat, that the big steelies lay.

It was there that I found a naked girl floating ass up at twilight.

Now it wouldn't be especially shocking to find a corpse in the Monongahela at Pittsburgh or the Anacostia at the District of Columbia. Dead people, after all, are the jetsam of cities and civilization. We love cities and we hate them. We say they are doomed yet we embrace them. The North Umpqua is different. It has a purity that makes a floating corpse especially ugly, an affront to decent people and a violation of propriety.

The inhabitants of Ernest Hemingway's Left Bank may change from generation to generation, twisted by history and fashion, but not the Douglas fir of Zane Grey's river. The North Umpqua is permanent, immutable. The evergreens still smell the same as they did in 1927. The mosquitoes slap the same.

It's hard to imagine any water being clearer or colder than the North Umpqua in the springtime. The drift itself—located downstream from the creek of the same name—is more than a hundred yards long and tails dogleg left into a series of swift channels as it moves downriver. The water in the drift is deep and rolling; it wells up from primal sources of the river. It's best fished from a shelf on the south bank that varies from fifteen to thirty yards wide. The water that sweeps across the shelf is waist-deep and so cold it takes your breath away.

Fishing at Steamboat is for those who know how. It's a privilege and a pleasure, a lovely memory for old men facing the long nights of December.

The road to Steamboat flanks the north bank and follows the twists and turns of the river higher and higher into the Cascades, deeper and deeper into forests of virgin Douglas fir. A few tourists on their way to Crater Lake use the highway, turning east from Roseburg at the interstate. But mostly it is used by fishermen and by loggers with strapping suspenders and too many Y chromosomes. The loggers horse their big Whites and Macks down the highway at breathtaking speeds. They own the highway by right of mass and muscle.

I don't know what I was doing there in the first place. I'm the kind of guy who wades around in shorts and tennis shoes trying to go one-on-one with hypothermia. Nobody wears tennis shoes at Steamboat, except maybe an escapee from a farm pond. It isn't done. So I borrowed a pair of chest waders from my brother-in-law, a surgeon who has a few bucks. I was entertaining one of his colleagues, a man from Chicago who specialized in diseases of the rich. I even brought along my Irish walking hat—a real prize—so that I looked like a mannequin at Norm Thompson's in Portland. My companion, whose name was Floyd, walked into Norm's and bought a pair of $80 waders, the kind that float if you slip in the water. He also bought himself a $180 carbon fly rod, the kind the professionals use in the *Field and Stream* stories.

Let it be said that on this occasion he didn't catch any more steelhead than I did. Part of the reason was he didn't know a whole lot about steelhead. I tried to help him out, but he wouldn't listen; some people are like that. What do you do?

What he needed to know is that steelhead don't eat when they make their spawning runs. They're said to strike at something just because it's there and annoying. That accounts for steelhead lures being particularly obnoxious—colored silver and gold and fluorescent green and orange. Steelhead flies are likewise large, gaudy, and often wrapped with silver thread.

He also should have known that steelhead won't hit a lure or a fly, but instead will mouth it and spit it out. So you get a nudge and not a hit. You have to pay attention. I think Floyd expected a fish to hit his fly like a shark and take off for parts unknown while he posed, extra cool in his expensive outfit, and played the fish like he'd been doing it all his life.

You fool a trout with a fly that looks like the real thing. A trout will hit it and catch himself.

But steelhead are mean and wary. If they see your line, they won't even go through their mouthing routine. So you have to use tackle that's light for the size of the fish.

When I fish a place like Steamboat, I know there're fish in the water. There has to be or else all those grown men wouldn't gather there with their expensive gear.

I approach a drift like Steamboat with expectations of catching a trophy. I have great patience. I can nurse my fantasy for an entire day when it's obvious to all but fools that the fish aren't hitting. But I never give up. So it was on this day. For hours I sent those great bright flies tumbling into the rich green of Zane Grey's drift.

Nothing.

So there I was. I stood for hours in the cold water of the North Umpqua, feeling awkward and pretentious in my fancy borrowed boots. I sent that fly out there again and again and again, until my shoulder sagged from the effort, hoping against hope that a steelhead would take it and set out on one of those heart-thumping runs that sets the reel drag screaming and the blood surging.

When darkness settled over the river, I stayed with it, hoping that perseverance and blind luck might make up for skill. My friend and the fishermen with good sense had long since retreated to the warmth of the café above the tail of the drift. I was alone with the night sounds and the brooding shadows of Douglas fir on the sides of the river.

There was no traffic on the highway above the north bank. Just me and the bugs. Me and the mosquitoes. Me and the slight breeze that kicked up from the west. Me and Zane Grey's phantom fish. Me with my brother-in-law's waders cinched up tight around my chest. Me and the cold. Damned fool me.

I saw a log enter the head of the drift, riding low in the water, turning slowly this way and that. I watched the log pause for a moment at an eddy before it continued to glide silently down the drift.

I saw that the log had buttocks, legs, and a spine.

It was the North Umpqua that offered me the log's foot.

But it was me, jackass that I am, who stepped forward to accept it.

It was also me who stepped off the ledge and into the icy depths of the drift.

And it was me who held stubbornly onto the foot and forgot about the waders and forgot about the current.

My brother-in-law is not a bad sort, but his boots were not $80 jobs that float no matter what. Fill them up with water and they're like columns of concrete. He is a medical doctor, a surgeon. Why hadn't I complained? Why hadn't I invoked the name of my sister and forced him to buy better boots for me to borrow?

Too late.

When the water got by the belt cinched around my chest and under my armpits, it entered the waders like a sheepherder in a whorehouse. I let go of the log's foot and sank to the bottom like a sack of sand. It happened so fast that I hadn't let go of the made-in-Korea fly rod I had bought on sale in a supermarket. Corned beef hash in one aisle, fly rods the next. I let go of the rod with some regret—it had cost me twenty bucks—and attacked the snaps around my chest with a vengeance while I rolled and tumbled lazily along the bottom of Zane Grey's famous drift. I wriggled free at last and shot upward with pain shooting through my lungs.

I came up under the log, which seemed to be waiting for me in the darkness.

I hooked my arm around it, discovering in the process that it was a young woman, and headed for the lights of the café above the tail of the drift. Sensible men were up there drinking coffee and eating enormous chiliburgers heaped with grated cheese and chopped raw onions.

The coffee was farther away than I thought. As I got within twenty feet of the shore, I could feel the current take control. It was a masterful, sure current and would have its way. I struggled for a better grip on the body, which turned faceup. I could see her face as we swept past the lights of the café. I could have let go and should have, but I was momentarily confused. I clung stubbornly to her corpse as the two of us were carried silently and swiftly toward the terror of the rapids at the tail of the drift.

She was a brunet. Her shoulder-length hair floated back from a widow's peak in great, black, undulating folds. She had a slender face with a fine nose and full lips, parted slightly in death. Her eyes, separated by a neat bullet hole, were closed—a blessing the movies would have us believe is usual. The closed eyes gave her the appearance of being asleep. It is one of life's sweetest, most private, and most remembered moments to wake in the early hours of the morning and see a woman sleeping by your side. The quarrels and the hard times are past and she is there, trusting. The innocence is special.

That's how it was with the girl on the North Umpqua. I swallowed. I felt like a voyeur. If I could have apologized, I would have. But she was dead. I watched her and maybe fell a little in love.

It had begun to rain. The rain felt good. It was then that I realized that I wouldn't be making it to shore. Falling in love and feeling the rain were two pleasures I was to be denied. No man could survive the rapids in the dark. In the daytime when you could see the rocks up ahead, maybe. That was a fact that I assessed without emotion as the savage current tightened its grip on me. It was pulling. Pulling tighter. Pulling me to the rocks as we are all pulled from the moment of conception. Most people aren't aware of the current until they're in their mid-thirties and begin divorcing their spouses, turning to drink, worshiping strange gurus, or generally screwing up their lives.

There on the North Umpqua the years turned into seconds. There was no use getting excited; that wouldn't do any good. The end was near; it was as simple as that. I welcomed it, maybe—who knows? I was also trying to figure a way out. There had to be a way.

There was a way.

The body.

The corpse was buoyant. It apparently had air trapped in its lungs. I shifted the body underneath me and spread-eagled her so she wouldn't roll. I spread her arms and gripped each wrist. I pinned her legs together with my own and locked my feet beneath her ankles. I clutched her as tightly as I could and held my head to her chest for maximum protection. If it worked, it would result in life. My own.

And so it began.

Immediately below the drift the current quickens and the river splits into a series of channels that weave in and out like a tangle of roots. The channels are separated by narrow islands of jagged basalt. The river turns sharply to the left. After another hundred yards the current swings right again and the channels come together for the run at the narrows. Here the riverbed takes a precipitous thirty-degree drop and the water is forced through a chute no more than fifteen yards wide and bordered by rock walls.

The narrows and the channels are the reasons why the fishing is good at Steamboat. The fish rest in the drift after their struggle up the falls and white water.

A white-water enthusiast with the best equipment might test the channels were it not for the narrows. The narrows were out of the question.

The dead girl rode low in the water and was awkward to maneuver, but she was better than nothing. I peered over her forehead searching for basalt. The channels narrowed as the current quickened. My eyes were accustomed to the darkness by now. I saw a flash of white. Ahead and to the left. Water against stone. I let go with my right arm. Stroked hard and deep.

Rock zipped by.

Couldn't think. More rocks. Her skull snapped. Long hair in my eyes. I couldn't see. Her body shuddered.

Rock.

Rocks on either side.

The roar.

I could hear the awful roar.

The narrows.

I adjusted myself on the girl's torso. Her body was cold to the touch.

I held on.

The roar was louder.

The water swifter.

We were into it.

She rolled.

I held.

Again.

I held.

It was over.

We were plunging deep, deep into the head of another drift. It was finished. I was alive. I didn't know who she was, had never met her, but felt as close to her as I had to any woman in my life. I took her by the hair and, stroking with my left hand, pulled her to the highway side of the river.

The rain had increased to a downpour when I pulled her body onto the rocky shore. I turned her over. Her skull was split wide open in the back. Her rib cage was caved in and her spine was twisted at an odd angle. I squatted there in the rain and examined the girl I had met in the drift and had embraced in the face of death. There had been no formal introductions as at a church, cocktail party, or bar. The river had introduced us. She, a silent form in the North Umpqua. Me, a jerk who didn't know when to give up. She had asked me and I had stayed. Then she had protected me. I was alive.

It's not easy to explain how I felt. It was a matter of honor and of being civilized. What would one of Zane Grey's heroes have done?

He would have done what I now had to do. The right thing.

I stood up and took the long walk to the café at Steamboat.

CHAPTER

Floyd was having a beer at the bar when I stepped inside. He managed to look impressed with himself even sitting on a barstool. It takes a real ego to pull that off. He didn't see me enter, so I left him there. I probably shouldn't have been so hard on him. He probably had a domineering mother. Maybe he would trade his bank account not to be such a prig. Who knows?

The man I was interested in was a weathered cop who was having dinner with an older man and a younger man my age—in his early thirties. The younger man had a waxed handlebar moustache which he pulled with a nervous gesture when he saw me standing there soaking wet.

I introduced myself to the cop and told him my story. Douglas County Sheriff Philip Boylan was a big man in his late fifties with crewcut gray hair and pale blue eyes. He looked like he had been around the block, several of them in fact.

He didn't seem especially alarmed at what I told him. All in a day's work. "You got her up and out of the water so she won't be going anywhere?"

"Not unless they have body snatchers on the North Umpqua," I said.

"Well, then, you might as well have yourself something hot to eat while we wait for an ambulance and for the rain to let up. This here's Dr. Pete Lindbloom of Roseburg. He's been fishing for trout at Soda Springs with his son-in-law here. I'll phone for an ambulance. It'll take forty-five or fifty minutes for one to get here from Roseburg." Boylan got up and went outside.

It was clear the sheriff had forgotten the son-in-law's name.

"Dave Chambers," the son-in-law said, extending his hand.

I shook hands with Chambers and his father-in-law. Dr. Lindbloom, unlike Floyd, had obviously known bad times and good. He was a gentle person and I had an idea he was in medicine for the right reasons. The money he must have earned in his lifetime sat well with him. Better to have *him* examine the dead girl than an asshole like Floyd.

"That's quite a story," Lindbloom said. He regarded me with some curiosity over a spoonful of soup. He was a large man, close to seventy, with a hearing aid fitted into thick-rimmed glasses. It didn't seem to strike him as especially unusual that I had just shot a rapids on top of a dead girl with a bullet hole in her forehead. Maybe if you were a small-town doctor, stories like that didn't bother you anymore, having rescued babies from the wombs of fat women and marbles from the nostrils of frantic children.

More likely he was wondering what kind of fool would stay on the river after dark.

Chambers, on the other hand, wasn't used to such excitement. He looked wild-eyed and agitated. I knew he wanted to say something but wasn't sure what was appropriate under the circumstances. "Catch any fish?" he said at last and pulled at his moustache. I'll bet he had a sore upper lip after watching a tight football game. I couldn't believe he had asked that question. I don't think his father-in-law quite believed it either.

"Dave here likes to fish," Lindbloom said with a grin.

Chambers took a bite out of an extraordinary cheeseburger that featured a tremendous slice of raw onion. "I never catch anything, but I have a good time trying," he said. Apparently stories of shooting rapids on dead bodies meant little to him; the fishing was the thing.

I got the attention of the overweight blond waitress who had DIVORCED WITH THREE KIDS written all over her tired face. There were three things you couldn't miss with in a place like this: breakfast, cheeseburgers, and chiliburgers. I chose the latter, and by the time I got it, Sheriff Boylan had returned from his squad car with a leather notebook in hand.

"Can you describe the dead girl again for me, please?" Boylan studied an illegible scrawl on the notebook.

The chiliburger was good, but the cook was apparently an onion lover; it was heaped with chopped raw onions. I went through a description of the dead girl again.

Boylan listened, then closed the notebook as though he had closed the case. "Marsden," he said. "Katheryn Marsden, age thirty."

"How do you know for sure?" I asked.

"I don't. Fits the description, that's all. Her folks called this morning looking for her, and we don't get an overabundance of murdered girls in these parts."

"Katheryn Marsden," I said. I could see her face staring up at the darkness. Marsden?

Lindbloom, it was plain, knew something about Katheryn Marsden. His soupspoon stopped mid-slurp and he started to say something. His son-in-law would have volunteered it immediately, but Lindbloom was of a generation that had great respect for the law. He was no doubt concerned about cluttering up Boylan's mind with useless facts. The spoon continued to the mouth. Lindbloom didn't say anything.

"Do you know anything about her except her name?"

"Not much," said Boylan. "Her father is a Harvard professor who has been teaching at the University of Oregon this last year."

I saw that Lindbloom was on the verge of being overcome by Boylan's news. Chambers saw it too. Boylan was too busy playing the clear-thinking sheriff to notice genuine emotion.

We settled into an embarrassing silence. After two or three minutes Chambers cleared his throat.

"What's your line of work?" he asked me.

"I'm a private investigator," I said.

Boylan raised an eyebrow at that. Lindbloom appeared not to have heard anything. He sat there looking as though somebody had whacked him alongside the head with a sledge. Chambers said he had to go take a leak. I liked Chambers's style. There was a man you could get drunk with and never talk about politics, the weather, or guilt. I pitied his wife after the onion on that cheeseburger.

Floyd finally spotted me and hustled over to my table.

"Hey, buddy, where in the hell have you been?"

"I shot the rapids down there on a dead woman. She had a bullet hole square between her eyes."

"No, seriously, I mean. I was beginning to worry."

A real friend. It had been dark for two hours now. "I lost my brother-in-law's waders in the drift down there and this policeman here is going to help me find them."

Floyd looked at Boylan. "He's going to do what?" He spoke like Boylan didn't exist.

"Help me find my waders," I said. "No sense buying a new pair if the old ones are still down there." That's what you call western humor.

Floyd said he would wait at the bar. He said he would just get in the way down at the river. I knew he was rehearsing the story he would tell his friends in Chicago about how a hick cop from Oregon agreed to stumble around a river in the black of night looking for a pair of fishing boots.

The ambulance arrived quietly outside and the two attendants, Boylan, Chambers, Lindbloom, and I went down to the river where I left the body. Dr. Lindbloom took his little black bag with him.

The body was still there, face down. Lindbloom squatted and examined the mutilated remains of her hips and back.

Then he did a strange thing. He pulled back the cheeks of her ass and examined her rear. He arched his eyebrows but didn't say anything. I wondered what that was all about. Apparently his son-in-law did too.

"Pete's been a GP here in Roseburg for thirty years. Delivered almost four thousand babies, something like that."

I wondered what his having delivered four thousand babies had to do with his examination of the dead girl's nether parts. The answer was nothing. Chambers was talking to relieve his own embarrassment.

"What do you think, Doc?" asked Boylan.

"I think she's dead. She's got a bullet hole in her head and she isn't breathing."

Chambers retreated to the brush and we could hear him vomiting. The two attendants strapped the body to a litter and we began the climb back up to the highway. Before we parted, Lindbloom gave me a couple of pills from a little bottle.

"I can give you a shot if you'd like," he said. "You're going to want to sleep."

I should have taken him up on it. Some of those shots are lovely.

Floyd drove back to Roseburg by himself. Boylan took me back when he had everything he needed to know.

It was 10 P.M. when I got back to the motel. A reporter from the local rag was there, looking half-stewed. He was in his middle forties, divorced, I assumed, with a child somewhere, the memory of whom gnawed and tore at his insides. He had probably worked on newspapers for fifteen or twenty years and knew his stuff. That meant knowing this was a decent story for a shithole such as this. He ran the palm of his right hand over his head, which was bald halfway back. It was as though his nervous gesture had denuded the front part of his head.

"Now let me get this straight. You were fishing at Steamboat after dark when you spotted the body of a dead girl in the water. You stepped right on out there in chest waders and went immediately to the bottom. Am I right so far?" He looked at me in amazement.

"That's it."

"You managed to survive that and you came up under the body."

"Right again."

"And instead of getting the hell out of there, you tried to pull the body with you."

"Dumb. I know. I know."

"So that you were sucked into that awful rapids beneath the drift."

I nodded. I felt like an idiot.

"You ever been to Hawaii?" he asked.

"Worked on the papers in Honolulu for six years."

"Ever see little kids ride belly waves on styrofoam boards?"

I grinned. "Yeah, that's roughly what I did with the corpse. Only it was a bit more tricky, what with the rocks and the falls and all. It wasn't Kailua beach."

He shook his head. "What was it like?"

"What do you mean, *what was it like*? It was like trying to maneuver a 1939 Hudson on the San Diego Freeway."

That brought a grin. He looked at his notebook.

"Listen, the Hudson line's free. Steal it if you want."

"Boylan said you were a private detective from Seattle. What kind of work do you do?"

"I started out with all kinds of grand ideas. What it's boiled down to is runaway kids, departed husbands, wayward wives, and insurance fraud. This'll be a break from the routine."

The reporter looked puzzled. "What'll be a break from the routine?"

"Finding the girl's murderer."

He scribbled a quick note and looked up. "Why is that? I mean, why are you going to look for her murderer? Cops'll do that."

"Because she saved my life, and it was Zane Grey's drift."

He scratched his neck. "You sure you want this kind of stuff in the papers?"

I shrugged. "I don't know why not. Sometimes it's easier to smoke 'em out if they know you're coming after them. You get a story. I stir a little action."

"It's up to you," he said. "I guess I should also tell you I string for the *Oregonian*. Pick up a few spare bucks that way." He looked at his wristwatch. "Plenty of time to phone the story in; they won't be putting it to bed for another half hour."

"The wire services'll jump right on it, I suppose."

He made one more note on his pad. "I can't imagine they wouldn't. You'll probably be on every front page in the country before the day is finished." He folded his notebook and stood. "You're a real cowboy, Mr. Denson. Hope it turns out right for you."

It turned out that shooting my mouth off that night wasn't the brightest thing I ever did. His story would force me to see my pledge through whether I wanted to or not. It would cause dangerous grown men to begin following me. There would be no turning back.

In the end it would damn near kill me.

CHAPTER

The phone woke me up the next morning. I rolled over and looked at the clock: 6 A.M. My friend Floyd slept on in the next bed. I answered the phone. I had a clever opener: "Hello."

"Arthur Steiger here."

"So," I said.

"I'm with the *National Enquirer.*"

"What's a *National Enquirer?*"

"A newspaper, what do you think? The one at the check-out stand with the pictures of movie stars with big tits and predictions about Teddy Kennedy's future."

How could anybody be that serious at 6 A.M.? "You a string or just a bullshit artist?" I asked.

"String," said Steiger. He sounded a bit disappointed. Probably wanted me to think he was phoning long distance from the *Enquirer*'s newsroom down there in Florida. Or maybe had spent the night on a United flight to interview what was obviously a damned fool.

"So what do you do, Steiger, Bigfoot and flying saucers?"

"Well, yes, mostly. Every once in a while I stumble onto something good."

"Like the story in the *Oregonian* this morning?"

"Like that."

"AP move it over the wire last night?"

"Hell, yes. Helluva story. Shooting a rapids in death's embrace. Zane Grey's fishing hole. Dead girl staring at the stars. Promise to the dead to find her killer. And you being a private detective and all!"

"What's your usual racket?"

"Cops for the *Oregonian.* Listen, the *Enquirer*'s hot for this one. You'll be on every grocery-store checkout in the United States."

"They call you?"

"They don't sit on a story like this. One of those dudes with a British accent called."

"Arthur, do you scratch backs?"

"I don't understand."

"The *Enquirer*'s got bucks. For a hundred bucks I'll give you some great quotes. They'll be all yours. But before you telex your copy, you have to show your story to Leo Hankens on the sports desk. He's a friend and won't let you do anything too outrageous."

I wouldn't dream of pulling a stunt like that with a regular newspaper. But I wouldn't lose any sleep over the *National Enquirer.* I needed expense money while I investigated the girl's death.

Steiger thought it over. "I think it's a shitty deal, but if there's no other way—" He broke off.

"There's no other way."

The other end was silent.

"Well, do you want the quotes or not?"

"I want 'em."

I thought he would. I gave him a jazzed up version of what I'd given the bald-headed reporter.

"Listen, this sounds like a dictation to a rewrite man. You been in this business?"

"I rework some of my investigations for true confessions magazines, stuff like that."

"How about papers?"

"Few years," I said. "Honolulu, mostly; Seattle once."

"I was wondering," Steiger said.

"Remember, Leo Hankens."

"Leo and I drink beer next door."

I hung up. It was done. Every newspaper in the United States, including the *National Enquirer*, now had the story of the moron who shot white water on a dead girl. I left Floyd sleeping and went to a pancake house to have some coffee and see what the bald-headed man had phoned in to the *Oregonian*.

What he had come up with was a fun story if your taste runs to fools with borrowed fishing rods and few brains. The *Oregonian*'s rewrite man, no doubt enjoying the afterglow of a pitcher of beer he had consumed with a sandwich in the bar next door, must have been delighted. The bald-headed man led with my account of the body in the drift and wrote it from there.

The story was full of quotes from Douglas County Sheriff Philip Boylan. Boylan said this; Boylan said that. He had been closemouthed in the café at Steamboat, but apparently loosened up for the reporter. He still seemed sure the dead girl was Katheryn Marsden. She had been born on April 26, 1953, in Roseburg, Oregon. Her father, Dr. Anston Marsden, was a graduate of Roseburg High School, not to mention the University of California at Berkeley and Oxford University. The latter was the source of his Ph.D. Marsden was an associate professor of English at Harvard University. He had a summer home near Eugene and was a frequent visiting professor at the University of Oregon.

Katheryn lived in San Francisco and had joined her parents for a fishing trip on the North Umpqua. The Marsdens had called Boylan earlier in the day to report their daughter missing. A careful cop and not given to hysteria, Boylan decided to check out the situation himself before calling out a search party. He was to have met the Marsdens just north of Steamboat. They didn't show. He was thinking things over at the café when I walked in sopping wet.

Local boy made good. Now this.

What was I supposed to do? Start asking questions. If Marsden was a Roseburg boy, there was a chance he had relatives or boyhood friends in the area. Where?

The Douglas County Courthouse and Katheryn's birth certificate. Go from there. I was waiting when the doors opened at 9 A.M.

The county clerk was a pleasant, gray-haired lady somewhere in her fifties. Yes, she said, there would be a copy of Katheryn Marsden's birth certificate on file there as well as at the state capital in Salem. And yes, I could look at it. Which I did. The birth certificate didn't tell me anything new except for one thing: the attending physician was one Dr. P. D. Lindbloom. Pete Lindbloom of the screwball son-in-law. Sure enough, he was in the phone book as well: Dr. P. D. Lindbloom, *phys.*, *res.*

Lindbloom, it turned out, was semiretired—I guess that meant he checked out an occasional ailing testicle or something—and was glad to have a visitor. Not much to do, he said, except eat and water the flowers. The flowers looked good.

His wife, an attractive woman with silver hair, was fiddling with her flowers when I drove up in my Fiat. The good doctor, who must have weighed in at 220-odd pounds, was relaxing in a lawn chair. The two of us retreated to his study, which was paneled in walnut and lined with medical texts and historical novels.

"Well now, you wanted my help with something, Mr. Denson?" Lindbloom extracted a gorgeous little penknife from his trousers and began picking absently at his thumb.

"Yes, I want to find out who murdered that girl I found floating in the North Umpqua last night. The records at the courthouse say she was delivered by a Dr. P. D. Lindbloom. I assume that was you."

Lindbloom grinned.

"I was wondering if you might know anything about the girl or the Marsdens that might help me out."

"My son-in-law told you I have delivered almost four thousand babies. That's close. The precise number is three thousand eight hundred and ninety-seven babies. That's a lot of babies."

"Yes, it is," I said. I wondered where this was going to lead me, but I knew I had to be patient; Lindbloom was of the old school and enjoyed working up to his point.

"I started delivering babies in Kansas and then Montana before I moved to Roseburg after the war. From the very beginning, for each one of those babies, I kept a careful record of the length of labor, type of delivery, complications, defects, and so on. I had a medical professor tell me to do that. He said a physician can't profit from experience unless he knows what that experience was. Do you follow me?"

"Makes sense," I said.

He handed me a leather-bound volume from his desk. "This volume covers those births from 1950 until 1955. Take a look for yourself."

I thumbed through the volume. What he said was true. Lindbloom was a meticulous record keeper.

"I'm a GP, a small-town doctor. You get to know people

when you practice medicine in one place for as long as I've been here. Most of those babies, I don't remember. I'm getting old, you know. But there's one thing that I don't forget, and that's having delivered the daughter of someone like Anston Marsden. He was a graduate student at Oxford when Katheryn was born. She was born in April and Anston and his wife flew back to Roseburg from England so she could have the baby near friends. He had been my patient before he went off to school; many's the time I've stabbed him in the butt with a needle."

"So you remember delivering Katheryn?"

"How can I forget? You remember me pulling back the buttock of that poor dead girl last night?"

"I remember," I said. I didn't add that I was curious as to why.

Lindbloom turned in his swivel-top desk chair. "I delivered both of Anston Marsden's daughters. The oldest of the two had a dark red birthmark in the shape of a four-leaf clover on the inside of her left buttock. Judging from the deep red color, I'd say it was there to stay."

"So?"

"So when Sheriff Boylan said the girl might be Katheryn Marsden I thought of the birthmark. Marsden himself thought it was funny. Thought it might bring her luck one day."

"What about the girl last night?"

"She didn't have a birthmark."

"Why didn't you tell Boylan?"

"I wanted to check my records first, make sure I was right. I phoned his office a couple of times this morning, but he wasn't in. I'll have to give it another try after a while."

"What about the other sister?"

"Susan; she was three years younger. From what I hear she ran off with a Dutch artist when she was twenty-two years old and nobody has heard from her since. That's been about five years now."

"One more question. Do you think many people knew about the birthmark?"

"Anston and his wife thought it would be embarrassing to Katheryn so they decided to keep it to themselves. Of course I suppose there might be a young man somewhere who could tell you something about it. I wouldn't know about that." Lindbloom grinned.

That didn't leave me much to go on except that Boylan was wrong in his guess and I'd have to start from scratch. I thanked Lindbloom and left.

I drove to the office of the county coroner to have another look at the body myself. Maybe Lindbloom missed the birthmark in the darkness.

Philip Boylan was there, scratching his stomach. I asked him if there was anything new with the Marsden girl.

He pursed his lips, considering how much he should tell me. He had a murder on his hands and was on the front page of the *Oregonian.* "Her folks were here an hour ago, wanted to pick up her body."

Boylan looked honest enough. "Dr. and Mrs. Marsden?" I asked.

"That's what he called himself, doctor. He's a professor."

"Are the Marsdens still around?"

Boylan shrugged. "Maybe they're still around, I don't know. They said they had a hearse rented from Eugene. They identified the body and said they wanted to fly her back to Boston for burial."

I took a deep breath. "To Boston. They identified the body?"

Boylan looked at me like I was nuts. "Of course. They looked at the body and said it was their daughter Katheryn.

They oughta know their daughter when they see her."

"When did you tell them they could have the body?"

Boylan looked surprised. "When we're finished with it, of course. The county coroner examined the body and determined the bullet came from a small-caliber weapon, possibly a thirty-eight. He took the necessary photographs and established her time of death as three hours before she drifted in front of you at Steamboat." Here Boylan looked self-important. "But we haven't finished examining her for physical evidence yet." The last phrase sounded right; he was pleased.

"Who was here when Marsden showed up?" I asked.

"Well, I was. The kid in front was out horsing around somewhere. He hasn't been here all day." Boylan looked disgusted. "He's here on a government grant; the county only has to spring for half his salary. An 'intern' is what we're supposed to call him. All he cares about is squeezing pimples, talking about carburetors, and running his hand up the skirt of a waitress down the street. I had to see to a jackknifed truck after the Marsdens left."

"Did you know Marsden personally?"

"Never seen him in my life before today. Heard of him. Everybody here has. But I've only been here six years. Worked for the state police before that."

"How do you know Lindbloom so well?"

"Hemorrhoids."

"Hemorrhoids?"

"He's my doctor. Best in town as far as I'm concerned."

"What kind of identification did Marsden have?"

"Hell, he had everything. Harvard faculty card. Massachusetts driver's license. Card that said he belonged to something called the Modern Language Association. Had a wallet full of stuff."

"Anything with his picture on it?"

Boylan paused. He was wondering what I was getting at. Was I suggesting that he may have screwed up? He didn't for a second believe he had, but there was always that sickening possibility. It is the first instinct of a civil servant to protect his ass. Always protect your ass, that's the first rule.

"It all looked proper to me," he said.

Boylan picked at his front tooth with a fingernail and stared absently at the wall. He was probably trying to remember if there was a picture in Marsden's wallet full of cards.

"Mind if I have a look at the body?"

Boylan was relieved that I'd stopped asking him about Marsden's identification. "Sure," he said cheerfully. "The county bought a brand-new storage unit a couple of years ago. We've got six refrigerated trays that slide out of the wall. They're made in Sweden. The best in the world."

He opened the door to the examining room, which was unlocked.

It was a small room, but efficiently laid out for its size. There was a stainless-steel examining table with a trough around the outside to catch the fluids. Plastic blocks for the arms and legs were stacked neatly in the center of the table. There was a stainless-steel sink with a divider in the middle and a glass-enclosed cabinet for surgical tools and chemicals. The refrigerated trays took up one wall.

"The Marsden girl's in Number One here," said Boylan. He twisted the handle in front and the tray silently slid out.

It was empty. Boylan blinked.

He pulled the second tray. Empty. He blinked again but said nothing.

All six trays were empty. Katheryn Marsden's body was missing.

Sheriff Philip Boylan looked like somebody had plowed him in the face with a brick.

"You elected or appointed?" I asked.

"Jesus Christ, she's gone."

"I don't suppose the social workers will be placing an intern with you for a while."

"If that little bastard had been doing his job, none of this would have happened."

Boylan narrowed his eyes and pursed his mouth in what was meant to be a thoughtful expression. He had a scapegoat for the missing girl. The problem was how to sell that to the newspapers. This was probably his first murder. The eyes of Douglas County were upon him. Now the corpse was missing, stolen from under his very nose. If the girl had been a logger's daughter, it wouldn't have made much difference. But she wasn't. She was Anston Marsden's daughter. Roseburg only had one Anston Marsden, living proof they weren't all red-necks.

"You got any ideas?" He meant to sound like he was flattering me. The truth was he needed help.

I knew that and he knew I knew it.

He could help himself as far as I was concerned. "I don't know any more than you do now. But I'll keep in touch."

I left Boylan knowing I had a tough job ahead of me. If the girl in the river wasn't Katheryn Marsden, who was she? Were the people who identified her body really the Marsdens? Why would anybody want to steal a corpse?

I had a couple of hunches: One was that the real Katheryn had read about the dead girl and for some reason wasn't talking.

The other was that the people who picked up the body were not the Marsdens.

But who were they?

Now then, my task was a strange one. Of all the charming young women on the West Coast, there was one who had a red four-leaf clover on the inside of her left buttock.

The girl with the clover was the key to my puzzle. She would be easy enough to identify.

That much was to my advantage.

But it was also true that most young ladies are not given to dropping their trousers for examinations by passing detectives.

That much was to my disadvantage.

My success in bedding down women has always been okay, I guess, but not fabulous. I try. God knows I try. Yet I've always lacked the brass that results in tremulations of the organs. Gaming men like Floyd nearly always claim marvelous success in such matters. I don't know whether they're lying or not; I've always had my suspicions.

In any event I had to start pawing clover.

I had started the process by letting Arthur Steiger hype a story for the *National Enquirer.* The rest would be hard work.

I used a pay phone to call my answering service in Seattle. Emma answered. She has a voice that is the stuff of wet dreams but, alas, reads Kahlil Gibran. Emma had some messages for me—a whole lot of messages.

"The first call was from a man named Lefty Steinberg," Emma began. "He said he's an agent. Handles professional football players, movie actors, celebrities, and politicians. Said if you read *Time* magazine, you'll know who he is. He wants to handle your story. Said there's big money in it. Left his number."

"Oh, shit," I said.

"You want the rest?" Emma asked.

"Go on."

"The second was from a man named William Diamond. He says he's a ghostwriter. Said he's ghosted stuff for generals, United States senators, professional football players, movie actors, and one American President. He didn't say who the President was. Says he wants to accompany you on the investigation of the dead girl and write a book about it. Says there's big money in it. Left his number."

"Go on," I said.

"Then I got a call from a man named Joseph Swinn—that's spelled with two *n*'s. Mr. Swinn is an executive with ABC television. He says ABC wants to buy the rights to your story for a television movie. Says he can guarantee Elliott Gould to play you. Says there's big money in it. Left his number."

"Keep going."

"The fourth was from a woman—a Mrs. Margaret Kunnert of Lubbock, Texas. Said you were a pervert for riding that girl faceup through the rapids. Said a decent man would have turned her over. Said if you're a man, you'll call to apologize. Left her number."

"Did she say there was big money in it?"

"No, Mr. Denson, she didn't. Do you want me to finish the list?"

"By all means."

"Then, Mr. Denson, I got a call from a man who didn't give his name. He said if you try to find the girl's murderer, you're a dead man." Emma paused. I could hear her breathing on the other end. "Mr. Denson, we like you here at the answering service. Your work gives us lots of good stories. You don't think he means that, do you?"

Yes, I thought he meant it.

"No, he's probably some kind of nut," I said.

"Oh, that's good," said Emma. "You also got a call from a Professor Piper."

"Professor who?"

"Piper, Nicholas Piper. He says he is a professor of American studies at the University of Hawaii. He says he can sail, write poetry, speed-read in five languages, program a computer, and fillet a tuna for sashimi. That's just a starter, he says. Wants to know if you could use some help."

"You're bullshitting me!"

"That's what he said, Mr. Denson."

"For Chrissakes," I said.

"Mr. Denson, what's sashimi?"

"Raw fish—the Japanese eat it. Any more calls?"

"Just one, Mr. Denson."

"Let me have it."

"This one was from a young woman, sounded like. Said the girl in the newspapers is not Katheryn Marsden. The woman, the one who called, said her name is Margo. Said if you show up in San Francisco at a place called Dick's Ding Dong at eleven P.M. tomorrow night, she'll tell you everything you want to know."

"Dick's Ding Dong?"

Emma giggled. "Dick's Ding Dong. That's what she said."

"Did she leave a number?" I knew she wouldn't have.

"No, she didn't, Mr. Denson."

"Did *she* say there was big money in it?"

"No, Mr. Denson."

Those were all the calls, as if they weren't enough. I decided to take a walk, convinced that if by the grace of God a man should be blessed with something absolutely bizarre, something prurient, he could make a million bucks. Most men go their entire lives without such a stroke of luck. It is the makings of fame. Me, John Denson, who shot the rapids on the belly of an unfortunate dead girl. Me, John Denson, celebrity. Andy Warhol once said that every person in the United States would one day get an opportunity to be a celebrity for at least fifteen minutes.

It was my turn. I wasn't sure I wanted it.

I took a walk to a Safeway a couple of blocks away and bought a head of cauliflower, a half gallon of screw-top red, and a copy of the Roseburg *News-Review.* The half-bald man had had enough time to fill in the details missing from his hastily written *Oregonian* version. I needed to do a little thinking. It was time for John Denson to get a little creative.

I remember reading an interview with Salvador Dalí in *Playboy* magazine where the interviewer had been dumb enough to ask Dalí what made him feel creative.

"When I urinate or eat Camembert cheese," Dalí had replied.

My kind of guy. Class all the way. However, I lean to raw vegetables and screw-top. That and maybe a joint now and then. The red gives me a low-cost, decent buzz. The vegetables give me gas sometimes, especially cucumbers. And pot'll put me to sleep if I don't watch it.

Small vices, after all. What the hell?

When I was walking back to my motel, a pickup truck tried to flatten me, running up onto the sidewalk in the attempt. I managed to fling myself behind the corner of a hardware store. Ah, yes, the good John Denson, still breathing.

And I didn't break my jug of wine either.

CHAPTER

Floyd was out when I got back to the motel. I cracked the seal on my jug and settled down to my newspaper to see what the half-bald man had come up with.

Boy, oh, boy.

This wasn't one of those piss-ant stories that writes itself. No, the half-bald man had himself some goodies to play with. In a day when television hype has reduced the attention span of an entire generation to twenty-second takes, a story has to be pretty damn crazy to keep 'em reading. And this was a pretty damn crazy story: Man rides a *nekkid* woman through white water. Would you look at that, Clyde? It was a story the half-bald man would look back on at the end of the year and grin, a story that would make all Kiwanis meetings worth it.

Some writers are like fastball pitchers. Bob Fellers of the typewriter. Their prose is mean and hard. They'll try to horse a story by their readers. Nouns and verbs and not much more. Others are junk-ball artists. Whitey Fords. They'll send up knucklers, curves, sliders, sinkers, spitballs, fork balls.

You name it. And every once in a while you'll come across a Catfish Hunter of the typewriter. A writer who is controlled, accurate, and disciplined, yet loose, relaxed, and able to flow with the game. A writer who can make his readers feel what he wants them to feel.

This story was big-league stuff. Dan Rather, looking wry and amused, would use it for the kicker on the six o'clock news.

"And finally, a fishing story from the small town of Roseburg, Oregon. Last night a man named John Denson was fishing for steelhead in the North Umpqua River. He didn't catch any fish but did latch onto the nude body of a young woman that came floating by. In doing so he got caught by the current. In a harrowing episode that rivaled the best of the movie *Deliverance,* Denson rode the corpse through a killer rapids. And lived to tell about it."

This was a chance for the bald-headed man to flash his style for the rubes. It was pleasant to read his stuff. Pleasant because I could see him hunkered over his typewriter grinning and feeling good as the graphs rolled from his machine. Deadlines would mean nothing to him once he was rolling.

I had contradictory feelings once I started reading. I felt regret that I had quit the newspaper business as I had quit the intelligence business before that. I had the touch and everybody knew it. The days of *Front Page* had long since passed when I came along, but it was still fun. Then along came the chains with their efficiency experts, barbarous little bastards in pin-striped suits. They got rid of the fun. Fun was sin. They wanted profits.

I also had an odd feeling I had stumbled onto the big leagues in another game. It didn't take Sherlock Holmes to figure out the possibilities. There was a hell of a lot more at stake than a mangled quote. My reporter friend could blow a few quotes and no one would be the wiser.

Not so with me.

I was hip-deep in warm manure and sinking fast.

There were three stories there and they were rich with suggestion.

The lead story was the tale of a detective named John Denson, an untalented but persistent fisherman, who shot white water in the darkness on the body of a thirty-year-old graduate student named Katheryn Marsden. Katheryn was a candidate for the Ph.D. in English literature at the University of California, Berkeley. Her specialty, like her father's, was Elizabethan drama.

Anything having to do with Marsden was good copy in Oregon. He was what is known, in the business, as a "local boy." Local angles sell stories. Oregonians who had never heard of Henry Kissinger or John Kenneth Galbraith knew Anston Marsden was a Harvard professor. A Harvard professor ain't bad. Oregon once had Wayne Morse. Now it had the novelist Ken Kesey, who milked cows on his farm in Springfield, and Ursula Le Guin, who wrote science-fiction novels in Portland. There was the poet William Stafford. Then what? Anston Marsden was from Roseburg; he was one of them, living testimony that you can spend nine months of the year living in the rain in western Oregon and still wind up with a few brains. There could be a coup at the White House, but the Marsden story would still be hot copy in Oregon.

The second story—from the Associated Press—said Anston Marsden's residence in Cambridge, Massachusetts, and his summer home in Eugene had mysteriously burned to the ground in the night.

On the inside there was a sidebar that said the girl maybe wasn't Katheryn Marsden at all. Or so suggested Sheriff Philip Boylan. She might be somebody else, he said.

Might be!

That was interesting. Boylan wouldn't say why either, and that part was a bit cryptic for your average reader. Cryptic but tantalizing. A good tidbit. Was it her fingerprints? Why didn't he say so? Why sound mysterious? But what could he do, quote the gentle Dr. Lindbloom about buttocks and four-leaf clovers?

There were also some people out there, the good folks who impersonated Anston Marsden and his wife, who must be a bit chagrined. They must be wondering just how it was that this hick cop had discovered their ruse. It had all gone so beautifully. The obsequious cop who had been so impressed by a Harvard faculty card. "Yes, Dr. Marsden. . . . No, Dr. Marsden. . . . If there's anything we can do to help, Dr. Marsden. . . . We'll get her killer, you can bet on that, Dr. Marsden."

No, sir, they hadn't counted on that one.

But that wasn't all. Not by a long shot.

The editors had boxed a one-paragraph item intended to show fellow Oregonians how Marsden kept fast company. Anston Marsden, in a televised BBC debate over the identity of William Shakespeare, had charged a scholar named Sir Giles Twigg-Pritchart with being a British intelligence officer.

Sir Giles Twigg-Pritchart!

Marsden couldn't have known who he was taking on. He couldn't have. I did. So did the members of the international intelligence community, of which I was once a member.

I got in my Fiat and headed north on Interstate 5 to Eugene and the campus of the University of Oregon, an hour away. I hustled right along. It rained off and on. I saw two white-tailed doe and counted three red-tailed hawks. The hawks seemed always to be there, waiting, if not for Godot, then for a possum or a dog to get hit by a car.

I asked a graduate assistant in the library where I could find the microfilm machines. She apparently assumed I was a professor teaching on a Ph.D. ten years out of date and merely blinked when I asked the question. She patiently led me through a labyrinth of rooms like a farmer leading a cow to the barn.

"You know how to use these machines?"

"Of course." I looked offended. Then I remembered I had forgotten to check the *New York Times* index. I went and checked it, found what I wanted, and returned to find out I didn't know how to use the machine. A thin young lady in combat boots helped me out. She peered at me curiously through thick glasses. She felt sorry for me.

Everything I needed to know was in one story from London by a *Times*man named Anthony Jones:

Dr. Anston Marsden, a professor of English literature at Harvard University, created a sensation here yesterday by charging on a BBC television program that Sir Giles Twigg-Pritchart, a well-traveled Shakespearean scholar, has for years been a top British intelligence officer.

Dr. Marsden and Sir Giles were guests on a panel discussing a recently found and hotly disputed manuscript purported to be William Shakespeare's last play. The play, entitled Jonathan Claiborne, *and said to be based on the New World adventures of Sir Walter Raleigh, was allegedly found by a Goan student in an antique sea trunk. The student, Mr. Mohan Sayani, said he lost the manuscript after an encounter with a prostitute in the Waikiki tourist district.*

Mr. Sayani maintains that the trunk, passed down to him through generations of his seagoing ancestors, contained a metal plate inscribed with the name Edward de Vere.

Dr. Marsden argued that if the manuscript is genuine, it "would prove beyond a shadow of a doubt" the position of many scholars that De Vere, the Earl of Oxford and a favorite of the Elizabethan court, was the real William Shakespeare.

Sir Giles, a colorful British intellectual whose by-line appears regularly in the Times Literary Supplement, *replied, "Humbug. That's nonsense and you know it."*

The program was broadcast live with arrangements made for viewers to telephone in questions. The cameras panned onto Dr. Marsden, who made the observation that is causing a furor here in view of the fact that Sir Giles is scheduled for an appointment at Oxford in December.

"The humbug is Sir Giles," said Dr. Marsden. "It is a known fact in international intelligence circles that Twiggy here is a fraud. His service in Commonwealth universities in India, Singapore, Malaysia, and Hong Kong was a cover. He is now and has been for the last twenty years a senior British intelligence officer. His posturing as an expert on Shakespeare is ridiculous."

Dr. Marsden concluded by saying he knows undergraduates at Harvard who know more about Shakespeare than does Sir Giles.

Sir Giles rose from his seat and called Dr. Marsden "a bloody liar and a damned fool."

Journalists here say this is not the first time Dr. Marsden and Sir Giles have tangled. The two men have argued over Shakespeare's identity for years in British literary weeklies, in the Times Literary Supplement, *the* New York Times Book Review, *and any number of academic and scholarly journals.*

In the Manchester Guardian *last December, Sir Giles claimed Dr. Marsden was "a perfect example of the ignorant philistines that pass for scholars in America."*

Dr. Marsden later replied that Sir Giles possessed "a second-rate mind gone to seed, a perfect example of how the British class system perpetuates mediocrity."

Although scholars do concede that Sir Giles is a generalist in an age of specialists, he is exceedingly popular. As a young man he earned a reputation as a skilled batsman on the cricket pitch. Somewhat harmful to his denials of Mars-

den's charges, during the war Twigg-Pritchart was known as a precocious intelligence adviser to Winston Churchill.

British scholars are eager to recover Jonathan Claiborne *to test its authenticity, but are dismayed by the bidding war begun by American universities. Harvard University has offered $750,000 for the manuscript—if it turns out to be genuine. The University of Texas, blessed by oil money, recently doubled the ante to $1.5 million—again if the manuscript is not fraudulent.*

Dr. Marsden has performed a computer analysis of Shakespeare's works and poetry acknowledged to have been written by De Vere as a young man. He said the results prove conclusively that the Earl was Shakespeare.

Dr. Marsden said the De Vere thesis was first proposed and documented by a man named J. Thomas Looney (pronounced "Loney") in 1920. Looney and a number of others—including Sigmund Frèud in 1937—have argued that the Shakespeare of Stratford-upon-Avon was a stand-in paid by De Vere and others who wanted to see the Earl's gifted imagination released from the constraints of the Elizabethan court.

A reporter for the Evening Standard *quoted Sir Giles as saying he would "personally see to it that the damned thing* (Jonathan Claiborne) *was destroyed." Mr. Twigg-Pritchart later denied the quote.*

The Times *asked him if he would like to see Her Majesty's Government obtain the play for the British Museum.*

"That will never happen," said Sir Giles. He declined further comment.

Marsden's charges on the BBC, coupled with Sir Giles's heated comments, it is said, have all but destroyed his appointment to Oxford, where he received his doctoral degree in 1953.

This is complicated by a rumor in London that Sir Giles's acquaintances in British intelligence have agreed to make sure the manuscript—whether it is genuine or bogus—never sees the light of day.

A BBC interviewer asked Twigg-Pritchart about that rumor yesterday.

Sir Giles had no comment.

Good God, Sir Giles Twigg-Pritchart was the very last man on earth who anyone with half a brain would want as an enemy. And for Anston Marsden to choose the BBC as the way to smash Sir Giles's career as an intelligence officer, challenge his reputation as a Shakespearean scholar, and ruin his appointment at Oxford was an act of bravado that bordered on the insane. I'd heard that scholars sometimes had bizarre egos, but Marsden was something else. His BBC stunt certainly wasn't good old American kick-'em-where-it-hurts street fighting; it was coming on like Genghis Khan.

I was curious about the guru who could inspire such fervor. I headed for the card catalog to see what J. Thomas Looney, pronounced "Loney," had to say on the matter. There were about two inches of cards after the heading SHAKESPEARE, IDENTITY. When I got to the stacks, I found Looney's book missing. But in an anthology there was an article by him called "Who was William Shakespeare?" In separate articles, Christopher Marlowe-champions, Samuel Johnson-supporters, and all the rest made their pitches.

I thought Looney's argument was very good indeed.

Looney said the historically accepted Shakespeare was a man christened Gulielmus Shaksper at Stratford-upon-Avon in 1564. The very same lad was married eighteen years later as Shaxper on one document and Shagspere on another.

There are, said Looney, six known signatures by this Shakespeare. Three are incomplete and three are on his will; the latter executed with difficulty. "By me, William" was scrawled on the last attempt, followed by a "Shakespeare" in a different and more proficient hand. This Shakespeare, the son of a glover, had no formal education yet wrote from the perspective of a nobleman. Furthermore, Shakespeare was widely read in Latin and Greek classics, was acquainted with the names and politics of the French and Danish courts. He knew the Italian language and culture and was intimately familiar with towns in northern Italy. He was well versed in military tactics, sailing, medicine, human physiology, mathematics, and mentioned, in the course of his work, some two hundred plants, sixty birds, and eighty-five animals of one sort or another. His vocabulary was estimated to have run from eighteen to twenty-five thousand words—at the lean end, more than twice the vocabulary of John Milton.

Looney found it odd that there was no recorded mention by any of Shakespeare's contemporaries, public figures, writers, or poets, of having seen, met, or conversed with this acknowledged genius and at his death there were no eulogies written—nothing.

I could see where Marsden might find *that* hard to swallow.

The real Shakespeare, said Looney, was one Edward de Vere, Earl of Oxford, a favorite of the Elizabethan court who was suggested by some to have enjoyed intimacies with Elizabeth herself. The Earl had two homes on the river Avon, not to mention an AB from Cambridge and an AM from Oxford. He inherited a company of actors from his father at age thirteen. He later had two companies and held a lease on Blackfriars Theater. He traveled on the Continent and thoroughly enjoyed Italy. He served in the military, campaigned in Scotland, and commanded his own ship in the battle of the Armada.

The Earl was also a poet, but because of his class and his status as premier Earl in Elizabeth's court, he dared not poke fun at Peers of the Realm and Elizabeth herself, as Shakespeare occasionally did. He was a poet, it should be added, until age twenty-six. In that year he was said to have been addressed by a man named Gabriel Harvey, in Latin and in Elizabeth's presence, with these words: "Thine eyes flash fire, thy countenance shakes a spear; who would not swear that Achilles had come to life again? . . . Thy splendid fame great Earl demands . . . the service of a poet possessing lofty eloquence . . . Mars will obey thee. Pallas striking her shield with her spearshaft will attend thee."

Thereafter, said Looney, poems signed by Edward de Vere disappear.

So a student from Goa claims to have found a play by Shakespeare in a sea trunk belonging to Edward de Vere. Oh, boy. Here I thought all that really matters are friends, good times, a full belly, a little screw-top, and a lay now and then—not necessarily in that order.

I was hungry so I decided to have a sandwich before I drove back to Roseburg.

I headed for fast-food and bookstore row on Thirteenth Street just west of campus. The most interesting place was Whitman's Beard about a half mile away; there was a chance it was outside the dry zone that surrounded the campus. I assumed Walt was the Whitman in question. It was. The Beard was also wet.

The girl behind the counter was overweight, cursed by pimples, and wore one of the damnedest getups I had ever seen. Her red skirt was too short and showed thighs with jellied fat. She wore cowboy boots and a see-through T-shirt. The slogan on the front didn't say much when taken out of context: M&M'S, THEY MELT IN YOUR MOUTH, NOT IN YOUR HAND. The humor came in her chocolate-brown nipples that stood out in relief like Everest and K-2.

The menu, painted on the wall, was written in code.

" 'Whitman's Whopper,' what's that?" I asked. It was worth a try; it only cost a buck and a half.

"A foot-long hot dog with mustard and chopped onions," said M&M's.

"How about 'Leaves of Grass'?" That went for a buck eighty.

"That's our veggie special: alfalfa sprouts, avocado, onions, tomato, three kinds of cheese, and mayonnaise. You can't miss."

"Looks like old Walt ran a few cows in his pasture?"

"What?" She looked vague.

"Sounds good, I'll take one."

"I'll give a call."

I was treated to two sets of intellectual conversation while I waited for my Leaves of Grass. Two bearded young men were earnestly discussing foreign policy. Two young women were discussing the treatment of artists in America and Russia. One wore her hair Joan Baez straight; the other, Afro frizzly. The men drank espresso coffee. The ladies shared a pitcher of beer.

"What it is, man, is realpolitik," said one young man. He blew meaningfully on his cup of coffee.

The other considered that, looking thoughtful. "Realpolitik," he said. "Hopefully, one utilizes indices of viable parameters. The problem is input; input is crucial, as you know. But who participates in the interface? You certainly don't want the media involved. I don't think anybody really knows all the ramifications. You have to be cognizant of that. It's all very problematic."

He had his lingo down pat, I'll give him that. But I didn't know what he said. It was better than the Japanese code. I couldn't take it; I tuned in on the girls.

"That's shit!" Afro said. She narrowed her eyes.

"I don't understand," said Joan Baez. "What about Solzhenitsyn, Sakharov, and all those others? They threw them in Siberian labor camps. That proves respect for poets and intellectuals?" She looked bewildered.

"Hah!" said Afro frizzly triumphantly. "You've proven my point!"

"What's that?" said Joan. She looked confused. "I still don't understand."

"Of course you don't. You have a bourgeois mind. The very fact the Communists go to the trouble to throw them in jail proves they think poets are important. Otherwise, why bother? In America we just ignore them. That's far worse."

I was waiting for Joan to pour the pitcher of beer over Afro's head, but she didn't. Instead she said, "That's an interesting point."

"But dumb," I mumbled to myself.

"Your Leaves is ready," M&M called.

"Who asked your opinion, you son of a bitch?" Afro said vehemently as I went to pick up my sandwich.

"Can you put that in a paper bag to go?" I thought I'd better eat it on the way. Afro was really getting worked up. She was a blonde with pale skin and blue eyes. The Afro must have cost a bundle.

I felt like a jerk for having said anything. Who did she hurt? And if she felt guilty for having a few bucks, what did it matter? She'd grow out of it one day and marry an accountant.

The veggie sandwich was good and didn't drip while I drove. But I think the alfalfa sprouts were domestic, not imported. I was in my Roseburg motel seventy-five minutes later.

CHAPTER

Comes now the first of my visitors. This one was the antithesis of that little fairy, Joel Cairo, who tried to push Sam Spade around. This guy could push anybody around he wanted. I could see it in his eyes when I answered the door.

There he stood in a blue suit of a conservative cut, a shirt with a hint of color, a proper necktie, and black wing-tip oxfords.

He flashed some boxtops. "My name is Andrew Carder of the FBI," he said.

"Oh?"

"Yes, may I have a minute of your time to ask you some questions about that unfortunate girl on the North Umpqua?"

"And about Bill Shakespeare's play." I said.

"We're interested in the play as well," he said. He hesitated for a second. "How did you know about the play?"

"It was in the papers this morning."

"Oh, oh, I see."

"Mind if I have another look at your Post Toasties?"

"Beg your pardon?"

"Your boxtops."

"Certainly." He handed them over.

"Okay if I check these out with a call to the Portland field office?"

He was a cool one, this Andrew Carder or whatever his name was. "That wouldn't do any good, I'm afraid. I'm working out of Salt Lake."

Carder was not an FBI agent, but he played in a fast league. His fake boxtops were perfect. But the number wouldn't check out with the FBI's computer list, a list instantly available to every field office in the country. He should know that.

No, this man was a bullshit artist. A bloody Englishman.

"No big deal," I said. "I believe you. It's just that the story in the paper this morning gave me the jumps. Won't you have a seat?"

He sat. I sat.

"Yes, this is a complicated case," he agreed.

"How can I help?"

"Was this the first you had heard about the manuscript?"

"Yes, it was. Would you like a glass of zinfandel? I've got some California screw-top here. Good stuff. Give you a cheap buzz."

Carder took a notebook out of his pocket and scribbled a note. He had his act down pat.

"You read about it in the paper this morning?"

"That's it."

"What do you know about Philip Boylan?" he asked.

"Not much. He's the county sheriff."

"You don't know anything more about him?"

"No."

"When did you first meet him?"

"At the café at Steamboat after I shot the rapids on that dead girl."

"Do you mind me saying that your reported encounter with that body strains credibility?"

"No, I don't mind," I said.

"Did Boylan tell you what he was doing up there on the river that night?"

I wondered why he was so interested in Boylan. "I assumed he was up there checking fishing licenses or something. I don't know."

Carder took another note.

"Well, I think that should do it," he said. He put his pad back into his jacket pocket.

I debated my next move, then decided what the hell. "Listen," I said, "I don't have anything to do with your play. I never heard of it until this morning. My story of the girl at Steamboat is true. It's a point of honor with me to find out who killed her."

Carder thought that one over. "I don't get your drift," he said. I was certain the pun was unintended.

"Zane Grey," I said. "Say, can I ask you an honest question?"

He thought that one over, no doubt wondering who in the hell Zane Grey was. He ran his tongue over his teeth and grinned. "What do you want to know?"

"I've often wondered how the English run nets in friendly countries."

"What are you talking about?" I could see he was trying to suppress another grin.

"I'm talking about the fact that you're no more of an FBI agent than I am."

He turned serious again. He didn't know what to do. It had never occurred to him that I was one move ahead of him. "You've had too much zinfandel," he said.

"Listen, the FBI can't be so dumb as not to know you

people have dealt yourself in on the action. The whole thing's a circus. Why shouldn't you go for the play?"

Carder laughed. He couldn't help it. "I believe I'd like a little wine after all."

I poured him a water glass of wine. I was sorry I didn't have some port.

"You really believe I'm an English agent?"

"Better than tending bar," I said.

He finished his wine in one long pull. "I'd better get going now. Thank you for your hospitality."

"Do you want to tell me why you're so interested in Boylan?"

Carder looked me square in the eye. "You can find that one out for yourself. I only have one word of advice."

"What's that?"

"You should bloody well stay away from that play if you know what's good for you."

It was probably good advice.

My next visitor was a carbon copy of the first. Same suit. Same shirt. Same shoes. Only his credentials checked out. A simple call to Portland took care of that.

His name was Lawrence Newton and he was impressed.

"Listen, I flashed intelligence corps boxtops for two years and nobody used the phone," I said.

Newton grinned. At least he didn't get pissed. A lot of agents regard their boxtops as the key to truth. A passport that guaranteed them the right to do anything they pleased. If you challenge them, they'll take it out on you. Newton, to his credit, wasn't one of those. He was in his late forties, which meant that he had no doubt served under J. Edgar Hoover.

"Mind if I ask you some questions?"

"Not at all," I said. "Have a seat."

As before, he sat and I sat. I didn't mind this. In fact it was a challenge for me to see if I could anticipate their moves.

His was straightforward enough.

"I want to know if you know anything about a missing Shakespearean play."

"Only what I read in the paper this morning. That's the first I'd heard of it."

"Is that true, the business about you and the girl and the rapids?"

"Sounds crazy, I know. But it happened, just like it said in the papers."

Newton shook his head. "You must have been scared pissless."

"That's about right."

"I want to know what you can tell me about Sheriff Philip Boylan." He watched me carefully when he asked that one.

"I'll tell you the same thing I told the Englishman who was here a half hour ago posing as an FBI agent," I said. I was, well, casual. It was hard for me not to grin.

Lawrence Newton almost messed his pants.

"The what?" His mouth literally hung open.

"He had a perfect set of counterfeit FBI boxtops. He wasn't a bad sort. Had a sense of humor."

"What did he want from you?"

"He wanted to know what I knew about Boylan and if I knew where Mohan Sayani's Shakespearean play might be."

"And what did you say?"

"What I told the newspaper reporter—the truth. I met Boylan at Steamboat after my fun on the river. And this morning I asked him about the dead girl."

"Asked him what?"

"If he was sure she was Katheryn Marsden."

"And what did he say?"

"He said Anston Marsden and his wife identified the body before it was stolen."

Newton looked disappointed. He was apparently looking for something I wasn't giving him.

"Could you describe the bogus agent for me?"

I did the best I could.

"He asked about Boylan too?"

"Sure did. Same questions as you."

Newton stared at the wall.

"Say, is it true that J. Edgar Hoover was gay?" I asked. Figured I would jolly things up.

Newton gave me a look. "Now, how in the hell would I know the answer to that?"

"Just wondered," I said.

"So you're a licensed private investigator," he said.

"Been doing your homework." Quick wit, Denson.

"I'll tell you what, John Denson. My advice to you would be to go on back to Seattle and take pictures of unfaithful wives or whatever it is that types like you do. Don't try to come on like a knight in shining armor. That girl in the river is very dead. There's nothing you can do about it. If you keep nosing around, you're apt to wind up the same way."

"Big leagues?" I was thinking it was impossible to be very dead. Dead, yes. Very dead, no.

"Big leagues," Newton said.

"There's money offered for the play."

"You'll never see a dime of it, Mr. Denson." Newton stood up and offered me his hand.

I accepted it. He was a decent-enough sort, I guess.

"You know you haven't seen the last of me," I said.

"I know and I think you're nuts."

"You're not the first person to tell me that, although

I'm not sure J. Edgar Hoover would have approved of such a crass expression."

He shook his head. Defender of the faith. Agent of the law. Wearer of wing-tip oxfords. Lawrence Newton left to tell his superiors about the British agent.

When Newton left, I took a little drive to pick up a half gallon of zinfandel, another head of cauliflower, and some smoked fish. I also paid a visit to the Roseburg *News-Review*. The *News-Review* wasn't exactly *The New York Times*, but it did the best it could with limited resources. One of the pleasures of reading newspapers is that they aren't all the same like beer, automobiles, and franchised fast food. Some of them are just plain awful, but they're a delight to read. Newspapers are a lot like women that way.

A man doesn't get appointed county sheriff without it being a big deal for the newspaper. Not much of a story, but a break from the Rotarians.

The problem was that newspaper librarians don't like outsiders scrounging through their clips. A pain in the rear. My mark was a plump lady, fortyish, with glasses hanging around her neck by a silver cord. I took a deep breath and plunged into my pitch.

"My name is Newgate Holt and I'm a graduate student at the University of Oregon. I'm doing my doctoral dissertation on the history of law enforcement in southwestern Oregon from 1950 to the present. The title will be: Parameters of Legal Personnel in a Typical Western State, a Comparison with the Frontier Lawman; Theories and Tentative Conclusions. The data will of course be available via computer printout for the press." I said all that with a perfectly straight face.

The plump librarian blinked.

"What is it you want?" she asked. Now she was perfectly aware, without thinking of it in so many words, that science is the religion of the twentieth century. Here I was, one of the priests whose business it is to squander her tax dollars with jackass studies just as Mayan religious men demanded the hearts of virgins. How could she turn me down? To do that would be to spit in the eye of science, truth, and progress. It didn't make any difference that nobody, certainly no reporter in his right mind, would ever be interested in such a ridiculous project.

"I would like to see your clips on Sheriff Philip Boylan."

The plump lady disappeared for a few minutes and returned with a bundle of clips held together with a rubber band.

What I wanted would be among the latest stories.

It didn't take me long to figure out why the Englishman and Lawrence Newton were interested in Boylan.

Almost everything I wanted to know was included in an article in the Honolulu *Advertiser* written by a reporter named William Orr. Billy Orr was a pal of mine when I wrote for the *Advertiser.* It had wound up in the *News-Review* library via a clipping service because Boylan was identified as a Roseburg man.

Philip Boylan, the divorced father of two daughters in their early twenties, had gone to Hawaii six weeks earlier on a vacation he had won on a radio station contest. He had checked into Pele's Embrace, the same hotel where a young man named Mohan Sayani claimed to have been mugged by a prostitute. According to hotel records, Boylan checked into Sayani's room just thirty minutes after the confused young Mohan had checked out. Sayani said he lost what may have been a missing Shakespearean manuscript in the briefcase as well as his wallet. He said he hadn't thought to search the room thoroughly before he left.

The Honolulu police asked Boylan if he had found any manuscript or briefcase in the room and he said no, nothing.

The hotel manager questioned the accuracy of Sayani's story. He said Pele's Embrace was a family-type hotel.

"Did you find what you want?" asked the plump librarian. Nice lady.

"Everything I need and I suspect a whole lot more," I said. That was an understatement. I thought I had a fair idea of the players and the game. Now I wasn't sure of anything.

"Are you sure?" she asked. I must have looked a bit wild-eyed.

"I was just trying to figure out how to program it, that's all."

She nodded gravely. It is the age of the computer. It is understood by the most simpleminded that a truth not expressed in numbers is no truth at all.

So Billy Orr had covered the story of the missing play by Shakespeare. It was time to call an old pal. I headed back to my motel. I setted down by the phone with the cauliflower, a glass of screw-top, and my telephone credit card. A large part of my business is chasing down runaway kids. That requires a lot of telephone calls to be billed to clients.

I called the Honolulu *Advertiser,* the morning paper in Honolulu said to have once employed Edgar Rice Burroughs as a reporter, not to mention John Denson. The whispering, hollow sound of the long-distance connection was soon interrupted by a familiar voice: "*Advertiser* city desk." It was Bob Gaines, who had replaced the purged Bernstein as city editor.

"Listen, have I ever got a story for you. The people at Queen's Medical Center have isolated a virus brought over by some tourists from Osaka. They're keeping it a secret, but in a week everybody on the island, and I mean everybody, will be sitting on the john. There won't be enough toilet paper to go around."

"Denson."

I giggled.

"Everybody here's been laughing their asses off about you and that rapids episode. Is that true or a lot of bullshit? Where are you?"

"It's true, and I'm in Roseburg, Oregon. They got lumberjacks here pick their teeth with Douglas fir. I want to talk to Billy Orr. Is he around?"

I heard Gaines announce to the city room that John Denson was on the line. Then he shouted Orr's name. "Listen, it might be a while with Billy. He's around but he's hiding, as usual, to avoid doing anything. Still trying to play Philip Marlowe, eh?"

A woman's voice interrupted him on the line. "Hey, sleuth, I was thinking about you the other night. Made me horny as hell. Why did you leave so soon?" She giggled.

"What do you mean, *soon*, Mary? I waited in line for six years and didn't get my turn. Listen, has Gaines found Billy Orr?"

Another female voice was on the line. This one too was laughing. "Listen, John, are you bedding down lots of doe-eyed things with your big old smoking forty-four?"

"Oh, hell, yes."

"Your pal Billy Orr wanted to demonstrate what you must have looked like on top of that girl. Says he wanted me to be the girl because he likes my belly."

Mary Tuchman interrupted. "He told me you agreed, Irene. Said you two were going to use the top of his desk as the rapids."

"Listen, what about Billy Orr?" I asked.

"What about him?" asked Irene.

"I'm paying expensive long-distance rates, you hapa-haole sexpot. I want to talk to him."

"First you tell us the truth about what you did with that poor dead girl after you pulled her out of the water."

I heard Mary giggling on the other extension.

"You're disgusting, Irene," said Gaines, who had been listening in from the city desk.

"Isn't anybody going to get me Billy Orr?"

"The copyboy's retrieving him from the Columbia Inn. What do you want him for anyway?"

"I think this dead girl may have something to do with that business of the missing Shakespearean play. A story with Billy's by-line was sent to the local rag by a clipping service."

"You're in luck there. Billy drinks with Nick Piper, the professor at the university whose student lost the damn thing. Piper hangs out at The Willows."

"Hey, pal, still making it with corpses in white water?" Billy Orr at last.

"How are things at the round table?" The round table was the reporters' table at the Columbia Inn.

"Well, we still get puu puu now and then. Long rice and pork today. Kaneshiro's still raking it in. More pictures of jocks on the walls. . . . I've been trying to con Irene into reconstructing the scene with you on top of the girl in the rapids."

"Billy, I want you to tell me what you know about Nick Piper and that student of his, Sayani, and the play by Shakespeare. Gaines tells me you're a friend of Piper's. Just talk, don't worry about the phone bill. I'll find some way to charge it to a client."

Orr coughed. "Piper's a hell of a guy. Next time you're over here I want you to meet him. How these yo-yos landed him is a mystery. He came here from the University of Chicago about ten years back.

The kid's name is Mohan Sayani. His father is an academic in India somewhere. They were originally from Goa, which used to be a Portuguese colony on the west coast of India."

"Which was invaded by Indian troops about twenty years ago."

"I think it was in 1959. Anyway, the State Department gave Mohan a grant to study American culture at the East-West Center, which is how he met my friend Nick—poet, encyclopedic mind, cocksman, and former player of tennis with Enrico Fermi. I guess I should add here that Goans are traditionally fishermen and sailors. Nick says they have served as merchant seamen for centuries. French, Dutch, English, Italian, you name the flag, he said."

"I didn't know that."

"Neither did I. Sayani and Nick were drinking martinis one day at The Willows when Sayani told him he had inherited a sea chest from his grandfather, a sailor in the Goan tradition. He said it was an English sea chest. Apparently there are differences in style. People collect the damned things and so on."

"Like stamps."

Orr coughed again. "Yeah, I guess. Sayani needed more money for school, so he took it to an antique dealer for appraisal. The dealer tried to screw him, of course. He told him it was a style that dated from the late sixteenth century but was common among dealers and not worth much. Nick says Sayani is a sharpie and knew the dealer was feeding him a line. Anyway, he took it home and gave it a closer look. He discovered that it had a false bottom."

"A false bottom," I said.

"In that bottom there lay a play, apparently Elizabethan in style, signed by William Shakespeare."

"Hoo, boy!"

"That's what the kid thought. Anyway, he asked Nick if that could be *the* Shakespeare? Nick told me that was one of the all-time, show-stopping questions he'd ever had put to him. He ordered a double martini with a twist. Then, Nick said, Sayani added rather as an afterthought that the chest belonged to someone named Edward de Vere. It was engraved on a metal plate beneath the lock in front."

"The Earl of Oxford."

"Been doing your research, I see. Then Nick asked him if he could read the play."

"But Sayani told him he'd lost it."

"Right. He said he was taking a stroll down Kalakaua Avenue in Waikiki when a lovely young honey propositioned him. You know the kind, part-haole, part-Chinese, part-Hawaiian."

"I know the kind." Did I ever. Gorgeous things.

"Sayani said he had the manuscript in a leather briefcase along with some homework. As an aside here, Nick says Sayani is one of the most fastidious people he's ever met in his life. Sayani told him he was folding his trousers neatly onto a hanger when somebody clubbed him over the head and lifted his wallet. Sayani got dressed and ran off without his briefcase."

"Folding his trousers neatly?"

"Folding his trousers neatly," Orr said.

"At a time like that I fling mine into the corner."

"Can you imagine?"

"Not really."

"That's when Nick phoned me and the people at the *Star Bulletin.* We had the story on the front page of our next editions, but it didn't help."

"Oh, boy."

"That's what Nick says. He says Sayani told him the play was a comedy. It was about the adventures of a certain Sir Jonathan Claiborne in the New World. In the Carolinas and in Virginia."

"Based on the adventures of Sir Walter Raleigh, the *Times* says."

"They got that from Nick."

"Now then, tell me about Sheriff Boylan."

Orr laughed. "Ah, the good sheriff. I suppose you know he won a trip here in a radio contest. He checked into a hotel called Pele's Embrace a few minutes after Sayani left. The Embrace is one of those older low-rise hotels that are being pushed out by the biggies. The rates are lower, but nobody takes care of them. That's the Embrace. The proprietor knew the girl with Sayani was a whore, but he won't admit it. She was probably a regular there. The cops don't know what to make of Boylan."

"What do you mean?"

"Well, he sounded innocent enough, looked bewildered and all that. The problem is that the story broke in the *Star Bulletin*'s late-afternoon street edition before the cops got around to checking the story. Those guys read Mickey Spillane anyway, what's Shakespeare to them?"

"Thanks, Billy, I think that's about all I need."

"What's this all about anyway?"

"I'm not sure. That girl I shot the rapids on was supposed to be the daughter of a Harvard professor who is an expert on Shakespearean manuscripts. When I went for help, who should be sitting in a café but Sheriff Boylan. See what I mean?"

Orr whistled.

"But that's not all."

"There's more?"

"It turns out the girl really wasn't the professor's daughter. But the professor turns up, says she is, and wants the body. Boylan says no. And a couple of hours later someone snatches the body from the morgue."

"Okay, okay, that's enough already."

"It's only the beginning. British intelligence agents might be mixed up in it; I can't tell for sure."

"I think I'll concentrate on Irene's belly. When are you coming over for a visit?"

"I don't know. When I have the time and a few bucks to spare."

"Mary says you'll be at the head of the line when you get here."

"I'm beginning to wonder if anybody ever gets to the head of the line."

"I've thought about that myself. Maybe her storied sexual favors are all myth. Take it easy, John, and drop a line sometime."

"Thanks, Billy." I hung up.

Well, I had to add Sheriff Philip Boylan to the list. The manuscript was central, of course. To think Boylan was an innocent victim of circumstance was to strain credibility. Maybe Boylan himself grabbed the body. He had the opportunity. He knew the kid out front was never around. But why, for Christ's sake?

Would a guy like Boylan know that a Harvard English professor was likely to belong to an organization called the Modern Language Association? I wouldn't think so. But you never can tell. It occurred to me that there might be a regular parade of FBI agents, representatives of foreign governments, private detectives, and other assorted bounty hunters following me around. I didn't even bother to try to spot them. To hell with them. The reason they were all poking around like randy dogs is that there was one thing that didn't make sense. None were stupid. Not one. The problem was that they were in the business of solving puzzles. Each piece has its place.

The thing that didn't make sense was my story about shooting the rapids on a dead body. That was bizarre. It wasn't believable.

If it wasn't believable, then I must be lying.

And if I was lying, then there had to be a reason.

The reason was that I was hiding something.

Maybe Bill Shakespeare's play.

I could have gone outside and waved them in for some wine. But I thought, Nuts, let them stay out there trying to look casual. Let them worry about who the other players are.

What I couldn't understand was why they cared so much about a play. Was the play really worth taking the life of that young woman I found floating in the North Umpqua River?

I determined, after a quart of zinfandel, that I would beat them.

The question was not who, or where, or what, but why?

I knew my participation in the mystery was annoying to the government professionals. It was annoying because I wasn't playing their game. I was asking different questions. I was in it for reasons they didn't understand. Reasons that didn't make any sense. If you don't understand how a man thinks, you can't predict his moves. That was essential in their business.

They had to know the moves.

Well, all this running around was getting me a trifle tuckered. What I needed was a good night's sleep before my run to San Francisco. I was in for much fun at Dick's Ding Dong—that much seemed certain. The way this business was going nothing would surprise me.

I didn't feel like explaining everything to Floyd, so I left him a note and found myself another motel. I needed a place out of the way of screwballs in pickup trucks. I settled on a place called the Douglas Inn that advertised cable television. I was good business for the folks at the Douglas; the Brit decided he needed a room there also, and so did the man from the FBI.

I had the better of the deal though. They had to watch my door to make sure I didn't take off. I got to drink a little screw-top and relax. The only thing I ever watch on the tube is sports—that and old movies. I was in luck that night—got to watch a first-rate soccer match between Frankfurt and Bayern Munich. After that there was the movie *Zulu*, with Stanley Baker and Michael Caine. Wow, what an adventure!

Every man needs a little adventure in his life.

CHAPTER

I slept late the next morning, had a leisurely breakfast, and took I-5 south to California. I had about an eight-hour drive to Dick's Ding Dong. Eight hours to the promised land. California meant gold in 1849. It meant the fantasy of Hollywood in the 1920's. Migrant workers from the dust bowl went there in search of work in the citrus groves during the Great Depression. In the 1940's California meant work in Lockheed factories. In the 1950's fortunes were made in southern California real estate. The beats, the last American bohemians, gathered in San Francisco in the 1950's to listen to Allen Ginsberg and Jack Kerouac.

In the 1960's California was whipped and twisted by a dizzying, psychedelic rush of fad. Who knows where it began? Perhaps with Mario Savio and the Free Speech movement at the University of California in 1964. Maybe with the flower children of Haight-Ashbury in 1967. There appeared leagues of wife swappers, transvestites, devil worshipers, and cults. Right-wingers stowed away machine guns and howitzers in Orange County while anarchists peed on the steps of city hall in San Francisco. On North Beach Carol Doda sported silicone breasts that looked like Cadillac bumpers while the voters elected a tap dancer named George Murphy to represent them in the United States Senate. Lesbians made love on stage while in the streets outside young people chanted themselves into trances in the name of Asian religions they did not understand. Charlatans, gurus, and amateur psychologists appeared everywhere, each with his special truth. Some truths were merely for sale, others cost more: a follower's ego, perhaps, or sessions of insults, abuse, humiliation, and flagellation.

California had come a long way from the Spanish dons and the jumping frogs of Calaveras County.

I didn't mind it as a spectator sport, but that was about it.

I wondered, as the Fiat's thirteen hundred cc's pushed me down I-5 South, what life would have been like as a cowboy on the American frontier. Short and harsh, no doubt. But I would have known what people expected and what was honorable. In a time when gurus and drugs were unknown, people took pleasure in such humdrum pastimes as smoking, drinking coffee, getting drunk, and copulating with the other sex.

Oh, well.

After a couple of hours, I pulled into a truck stop for gas and a cup of coffee. Besides that, I figured the folks following me might want to take a leak or something. I didn't have any reason to give them a hard time. Why should they have to pee in paper cups for no good reason?

When I pulled out of the truck stop, I could see them pulling in behind me. There was no way of knowing how many government agencies, foreign governments, and private nuts were involved. But I did know that if we had all turned on our headlights, we could have passed as a funeral procession.

I concentrated on the road, passing Medford and Ashland in Oregon, the Siskiyou Mountains, and descending into California. Passing Weed, Redding, and Red Bluff. Passing Willows and Williams. Coming at last to the Bay Area.

I made San Francisco in plenty of time.

Got myself a motel room which my new friends would take turns searching. I took a little nap, had some dinner, and headed for Dick's Ding Dong.

Here I was, a Zane Grey hero riding the canyons of the big city on behalf of William Shakespeare, Esquire.

Poor Bill.

Dick's Ding Dong was a gay bar. Up behind the bar where the Long Branch or Red Dog Saloon would have had a handsome mirror or paintings of naked ladies, Dick had a twelve-foot-long velvet penis. The velvet was peach colored. The penis had testicles covered by a furry shag rug. Dick must have been a fun guy; I have to admit his decor made me smile.

I sat there at the bar, a flagrant and no doubt awkward-looking heterosexual trying to look casual. It didn't matter if this was a watering hole for homosexuals, really; it wasn't much different from a lot of other places. The patrons routinely went to the john to take a few tokes on a joint. The music on the jukebox was by turns outrageous and randy. The idea was to grin a little and enjoy it now because it would be replaced next week anyway. As long as they don't bug me or pass a law against people reading books, who am I to complain? Hell, I smoke a little bud myself when it's handy.

One thing I really do like though, really go for, is honest

fashion. Nobody loves a lady's nipples under a thin T-shirt more than I do. Whenever I'm around bra-less girls in T-shirts, my testicles feel like baseballs underneath me.

So there I sat with my pitcher of Coors beer on that lazy afternoon, when a bearded young man invited me to his table. There was another young man at his table, together with a girl. The girl, it must be said, was a looker, but she didn't wear one of the aforementioned T-shirts. For all my differences with people of their generation, they are more civilized than I in one important respect: They're unafraid and even anxious to meet new people. That's sometimes put on, but is very often genuine. It is their passion for experience, I suppose, and that's not all bad.

"Would you like to join us?" asked the young man with the beard. It was a fine beard, red and thick. He had wire-rimmed spectacles that made him look like a student in St. Petersburg in 1917.

"Sure," I said. I sensed intuitively that his invitation had something to do with my rendezvous with Margo. I also sensed there would be no four-leaf clovers beneath the girl at the table. Whoever was setting this up no doubt knew how to read a newspaper. He or she knew people were being killed. I shook red-beard's hand with the interlocking thumbs bit.

"Name's Eric," he said.

"John Denson."

He was, as they say, mellow. That too was civilized.

His companion was named Allen, a brown-eyed young man with an Emiliano Zapata moustache. Handsome thing.

The girl was about five feet seven inches and 120 pounds. She had a soft, wide face and short brown hair. She wore blue jeans and a gray sweatshirt that zipped down the front.

Allen watched me as I leaned forward to shake her hand.

He grinned. "This is Helen," he said. We had one thing in common, Allen and me, we were both suckers for romance.

Helen had a melancholy look in her eyes that said she had once been poor and doomed. I had been there too. It would have been sweet to take her away in my Porsche, like Robert Redford. We would drive to my home in the Big Sur as the sun was setting crimson over the Pacific.

"John Denson," I heard myself saying. Her hand was soft.

"You look like your picture in the paper, Mr. Denson," she said. Her voice trailed off. She had been crying.

"Call me John, please." There was an uncertainty about her, a wariness that said she had given much in her life and received little in return.

"You were the one who called my answering service in Seattle?"

She shook her head. "A friend did."

"Ahh." I was certain she had no birthmark in the shape of a four-leaf clover. I didn't know what to say next, partly because I thought there was a hint of chemistry between us. Just a hint, that's all. The stuff of dreams. I didn't want to spoil it.

It must have been obvious because Eric was grinning like a horse's ass. Allen looked amused also.

I didn't want to push things. "How long you been in San Francisco?"

She started to smile, watching me carefully with her brown eyes. "How did you know that?"

"What?"

"That I'm not from San Francisco?"

I shrugged my shoulders. "Probably aren't many people who are from San Francisco. Most of them come from somewhere else, like you, following their dreams."

She closed her eyes. "Yakima."

I couldn't help laughing. "Made it a little easier to call, I bet, me being from Seattle and all."

She laughed too. "There was a little of that, I guess."

"You know William O. Douglas went to school in Yakima?"

"Who?"

"The Supreme Court justice. When Franklin Roosevelt appointed him to the court, the Yakima *Herald* ran an editorial titled YAKIMA NOT TO BLAME."

"He was the one who married the twenty-four-year-old girl."

"Well, there was that too. My dad served in his unit in World War One. When did you leave Yakima?"

She considered that for a moment, wondering perhaps how different things might have been had she stayed and married a hardware clerk or real-estate agent. And here she sat, in a San Francisco gay bar, talking to a man who knew about Yakima and seemed not to care.

"There were five of us kids. My father worked in a factory that made wooden fruit lugs. When he worked. Mostly he didn't. I went to a community college for two years and came here five years ago. Not much has happened since." She looked embarrassed.

Eric swallowed. Allen cleared his throat. Whatever else, they knew about life turned wrong.

"What the hell," I said. "I pitched watermelons in Hermiston, cut asparagus in Walla Walla, picked cherries in Prosser, hops in Sunnyside, and lived for a month in a 1949 Plymouth."

"What's your line, John?"

I looked surprised. "My line? You know my line. You read it in the newspapers. I'm a private investigator."

"We have to be sure," Helen said softly. She wanted me not to be a liar.

"Well, I once was an intelligence agent. After that I was a newspaper reporter." I rubbed my eyes. "Makes you wonder, doesn't it? Anyway, a few days ago I was fishing for steelhead in southwestern Oregon when a body floated by. Right in front of me. I tried to retrieve the body—it was a young woman—but we were sucked into the rapids. What the papers said was true. She was naked. She had a bullet hole between her eyes. I rolled on top of her and rode her corpse through the rocks. Cut her up like nothing you can imagine. I want to find her murderer."

"Why is that?" asked Zapata.

"She saved my life."

My companions said nothing, but I could feel the tension. I could feel three sets of eyes watching me, especially Helen's.

"Listen, I know it sounds strange. The police had a hard time believing me too. She looked innocent. Innocence is lovely. I don't know what she was in real life. I don't care. Maybe I can't explain how I feel. I do know I owe her my life. Simple justice means somebody has to find her killer. The cops will try, but what is she to them, after all? Another stiff. Since it's my business finding things out, I figured this one's on the house."

Helen swallowed.

"Listen, did that sound foolish or embarrassing?"

I looked at them one at a time. They knew I was on to their game. They had to make a decision.

Eric cleared his throat. He looked to the others. They believed me. They were sentimental. That I liked.

"We'll take you to Margo," said Eric.

We took a stroll down a very mean street indeed. Past bars where men drank alone. Past squalid theaters that showed movies of people inflicting pain on one another, that promised oral and anal sex, live onstage. Name your fantasy, pardner. Flickering neon lights promised everything. Hustlers, whores, pimps, and pitchmen. The darkest of our dark sides.

We turned in at last to a place called Bill's Bawdies. The Bawdies were girls who danced naked on a ramp in the middle of a room full of tables with tops the size of pie plates. The ramp itself was surrounded by a bar where customers were served from behind so they could look straight up at the ramp and examine the dancers' genitals at less than four feet.

No more than ten or twelve customers in the room drank beer that cost them a buck and a half a bottle. They nursed their drinks as they did their regrets. They were mostly middle-aged males. A few were convention-goers. They looked prosperous but doomed.

None of them had ever had a girl as gorgeous as the girl on the ramp and none of them ever would. That knowledge gnawed and ate at them. They wondered where girls like that had been when they were young. Desire overwhelmed them. The knowledge that such beauty existed and had passed them by tortured them.

There is one fact of life that is true of all men, I'm convinced. The cheat is that it's impossible to know all the attractive women, all of them in the entire world, to hold them tightly in a sweaty bed and smoke a cigarette or joint afterward and laugh a bit. The best these men can do is watch and dream of what might have been. Hell, it's the same with me; every time I see a girl with a tightly be-jeaned butt, I feel cheated.

They sat alone and watched that lovely girl moving inside her young skin. Each bore stolidly his private thoughts and the awful burden of middle age. The girl was lovely. She too would age one day. And there would be another, just as grand.

The girl on the ramp was a slender brunet. She had the most perfect behind I'd ever seen. But her posture was most incredible. The curve of her spine above her hips was sensuous in its promise. In bed it would bend like a willow. She was hardly dancing, moving aimlessly to music on a jukebox, when we walked into the room. I paused to let my eyes adjust to the darkness. The room smelled of stale beer and God knows what else. When she saw us, she picked up the tempo and followed us with her eyes. She had been crying, I could see it from a distance.

Eric led us to a table at the foot of the ramp where she danced. Colored discs rotated in front of lights mounted on the ceiling. The lights were trained on the brunet and changed from yellow to green to blue to red and back to yellow again.

Her eyes locked onto Helen's and Helen nodded.

That meant good news, apparently, because Margo grinned and really began to dance.

Her customers appreciated it. There wasn't much in it for them when she was just standing there, moving at random and staring at the blue cloud of cigarette smoke with a bored look. But now she kicked up her legs and really moved. She rotated her rear at the darkness and humped the cigarette smoke with her lips. And a fine sheen of perspiration highlighted the supple grace of her spine. She kicked her legs higher and higher, giving the johns a flash of what they were there to see.

At the crescendo of the song she did a slow, wide roll of her rump right above our table.

And there it was.

As sweet and as perfect as you please.

A little four-leaf clover on the inside of the lady's sweet cheek. I could see that Helen was watching me and grinning.

"Helluva behind, huh?" she said.

"I'm finding it a bit hard to breath," I admitted. Margo was Katheryn Marsden.

"Well, it's my turn up now. I'll show you how to move a behind," she said.

It was not until then that it dawned on me that Helen was a bottomless dancer too.

"That girl on the river?"

"Oriana," said Helen. "Oriana Kauffmann."

"Oriana. Was Oriana a bottomless dancer too?"

"Nobody could dance like her. Except Margo maybe. Right now I'm to go up there and give you a dance."

Before she left for the dressing room, Helen said something to Eric and he and Allen left. I was alone with my new clients.

When I saw Katheryn next, she was dressed in blue jeans and a Cal-Berkeley sweatshirt. She got herself a bottle of Coors and a glass and sat down beside me with an impish grin on her face.

"Pleased to meet you, John Denson."

I wanted to call her Katheryn but I thought better of it. "I can't recall when I've met such a charming person as yourself under conditions as spectacular as these," I said.

"Why, thank you, Mr. Denson." She blinked her eyes mock seductively.

"Call me John, and I'm partial to girls with a sense of humor."

By this time Helen had appeared onstage and was adjusting the machine that controlled the rotating colored lights above the ramp. She selected more colors and a faster tempo. She didn't have anything on except a pair of high-heeled shoes.

Helen punched a record on the jukebox to match the tempo of the lights and came on down the ramp to stand above Katheryn and me. I had to adjust myself. I think that's how the expression goes. I tried to disguise it as a casual adjusting of my trousers. But Katheryn knew better and grinned.

It's safe to say that nude dancing is one of the livelier of the lively arts. It's also fairly unsubtle. But when Helen walked down the ramp wearing nothing more than high-heeled shoes, she had only begun to strip. She proceeded to lay bare her heart as well as her body.

Katheryn's dancing had been patently, determinedly, doggedly erotic. She had every provocative gesture, every clichéd bump and grind down pat. But she was so good at it nobody cared. She danced with power, grace, and rhythm. Her pride in her body bordered on arrogance. She enjoyed her control over the poor bastards who watched from the smoky shadows. She worked looking constantly at them, seducing, offering, suggesting, teasing.

Helen was different. She was slender, fragile, and carried with her an air of vulnerability, of innocence displayed pitiably on the rack of the sordid ramp. To watch her thus exposed was to violate her.

Katheryn was a leader; Helen was a follower. Their scheme involving me, whatever it was, would be Katheryn's idea, but Helen would see her part through.

Up there on that awful ramp, Helen was by far the more erotic of the two.

When Helen's turn was up, the johns applauded vigorously. That was rare enough to turn the head of the bartender in the back of the room.

Later, when they got off work, Katheryn and Helen asked me to return to their apartment with them. Katheryn said we could discuss our arrangement there. I didn't know what she meant by that exactly.

It was a small apartment. It had a queen-sized bed in its only bedroom. It had a couch, a color television set, and a couple of chairs in the living room; a stove and a refrigerator in the kitchen. That was all. That and the john.

Katheryn turned on the television set when we got inside. It was 3 A.M. and there was a Japanese monster movie on an all-night station. The Japanese are good at monster movies. They have the imagination. And they like the technical challenge of creating mechanical monsters that look like the real thing.

I, as usual, was bewildered. "I thought we were going to talk about finding Oriana's killer," I said.

"Later," said Katheryn. "I think Helen needs you in the bedroom. Dancing gets her worked up. Sexual tension. She needs a comedown."

"Me?"

"You."

When I stepped into the bedroom, Helen looked just like she did on the dance ramp. Only she didn't have high heels on. I started to unbutton my shirt and I could hear the dubbed English of the movie in the next room. Seems there had been a radiation leak at a nuclear generator near Yokohama. A geisha who served wealthy industrialists had been passing by at the time and was transformed by the radiation into an enormous cancer that consumed everything in its path. A young scientist at the University of Tokyo was the geisha's cousin. They had played together as children and he wanted to put the cancer out of its misery. I felt silly as hell standing there listening to that with a naked lady awaiting me. But she was listening to it too and grinning. I opened the door and asked Katheryn if she could turn it down a trifle; she did, and I turned to get on with the task at hand.

"My God, this is a smorgasbord," I said when I looked

down on her. "All the marvels of God's creation and of such quality and in such quantity as to defy imagination. I don't know if I'm up to it."

Helen grinned. "You're already up to it."

"That's not what I mean."

"Do you know what I like to do when I go to a smorgasbord?"

"What's that?" I asked dutifully.

"I like to try everything out. I like to have a little bit of this and a little bit of that. You never know what's going to be good."

I was a bit startled by that coming from the small and exposed figure who had been on the ramp an hour earlier. "I'll do my best," I said.

"Better save room for more," she said and grinned.

"Well, I don't think we should put limits on it." With that I settled next to the softness of her body and one of life's beautiful pleasures. Helen was surprisingly uninhibited. She knew what would please me and wasn't at all bashful about letting me know her wants as well. I was a glutton. Tried everything.

By the time we finished, Katheryn was watching a World War II movie starring John Payne as a grimacing bead of sweat. Helen took first dibs on the shower and left the bedroom, leaving me under the sheets feeling weak and disbelieving. I was getting up to join the shower line when the door opened and there stood Katheryn. She had misplaced her pajamas somewhere and was giggling.

"What's this?" I asked.

"Helen said you didn't believe in limits."

It took me a second to understand what she was talking about. Professor Marsden's daughter was offering to go to bed with me. Why would she do that?

"I'll pass," I said. I was so startled by the openness and

generosity of her offer that I couldn't think of one single clever line.

Katheryn dangled one slender hand in front of her groin and just stood there, breathing.

I still didn't know what to say. "Listen, there shouldn't be any offense, but I'm prone to simply sleeping it off, maybe watching an old movie on the tube. Something like that." The truth is there was a difference between generations at work. Maybe I thought the idea of going to bed with Helen's friend thirty minutes after was perverse. Maybe I was worried about my image with Helen. Who knows? In any event, I couldn't do it.

Yet there she stood, breathing. She knew that's all it took. She knew how to work the johns from the dancing ramp. She knew how to work me there in the bedroom. All she had to do was stand there until my testicles took charge. "Listen, how much do you charge for a day of your kind of work?" she asked.

I tried like hell not to stare at that hand. "I get anywhere from a hundred to six hundred bucks a day plus expenses. It depends on the job and how much I think my client is able to pay." My mouth was dry. My penis stirred fitfully, like an uncertain Polish sausage.

"Helen and I are a little short on coin these days, but we still want to pay you for your troubles." Katheryn moved her hand to the swell of her hip.

My eyes followed her hand. I couldn't help it. They couldn't be doing this because of a fee. "I'll still pass, I think."

"Straight John Denson?"

"Straight John," I said.

"I suppose you'd prefer me to sleep on the couch as well."

"If you don't mind," I said. My heart was beating like kettledrums gone mad.

"Are you absolutely sure?" Katheryn was having a little fun with me now.

"I'm sure."

"Okay," she said as though she regretted it greatly. She slipped back into the living room. I stared at her rump as she left and felt a pang of regret. She had those swell little buns.

My mind was only partly on Katheryn when I settled back on the bed. Mohan Sayani. A sea trunk. *Jonathan Claiborne.* William Shakespeare. Edward de Vere. Dr. P. D. Lindbloom. A four-leaf clover. Philip Boylan. A stolen body. A British agent. An FBI agent. A twelve-foot velvet penis. A professor's daughter dancing naked onstage. Oriana Kauffmann.

Now this. Most men would walk on fire for what I was offered as a matter of course. Katheryn and Helen obviously had in mind one hell of an IOU. Was I supposed to launch a one-man assault against a brigade of murderers, body snatchers, bounty hunters, and intelligence agents, both foreign and domestic? Onward strode Denson, brave John Denson.

Helen returned from the shower and slid into bed beside me. "Margo tells me you weren't in the mood."

"I guess it was just too much for me. You were just fine, thanks."

Helen snuggled close. "Thank you," she said softly.

"I can't understand why you two tried that stunt anyway. What do you think I am?"

"A man. Margo did get that thing all worked up again, didn't she?"

"It runs on instinct, not brains."

"What are you going to do with it now?"

"Put it to use, I guess; it's not going to relax. I can take my shower later. I want to talk."

A hand moved onto my shoulder. "Talk."

"I want to talk to a person, not a thing."

The hand tightened.

"How is it that you wound up on that ramp, Helen?"

The hand relaxed, then began kneading my shoulder. Her voice was soft, almost a whisper. "I was used and thrown aside by four different men. I had tired feet from waitressing. I was lonely. I met Margo who said it was easy money. 'Just get out there and move around,' she said. She said after a while you forget they're out there watching." The hand moved under my arm and Helen held on. "The first time I did it, I got loaded with Margo beforehand. I was drunk and clumsy. The manager knew I was loaded. He said he understood and it would be easier the next time. It was. After a while I learned not to be embarrassed or to hate them. They're just there, that's all. Margo was right. I've been doing it eight months now and I haven't been with a man in all that time."

"That's a long, long way from Yakima."

I could feel her breathing against my shoulder. "It makes you wonder where we're all going, doesn't it?"

"Yes, it certainly does that," I said. "It's getting meaner every year."

"Have you ever walked in an alfalfa field just after it's been mown?"

I had. "Yes," I said.

"It smells like sweet tea."

She was right. "Yes, it does."

I felt something wet on my shoulder. Helen began to cry. "I wish you hadn't seen me dance."

"Maybe one day we'll go to the movies and eat popcorn."

Helen didn't say anything. After a while she fell asleep.

If I was curious why a Yakima girl would wind up naked on a dancer's ramp, I also had to wonder about Katheryn Marsden, who for some reason was calling herself Margo. She certainly had a choice. Why would she do that? If I thought I knew Helen a little, I never could say the same about Kathryn. She kept her distance always. She was wary, suspicious. That didn't bother me especially. I attributed it to her being smart and good looking and my being a bit of a flake.

I fell asleep; figured I could take my shower in the morning.

CHAPTER 7

The first thing I saw the next morning was Katheryn sitting in a chair drinking a cup of coffee. Then Helen came into the bedroom with two cups.

"Morning, Rip," she said.

"What century is this?" I asked. Always clever.

"No more than a day later." She gave me a cup of coffee as I squatted there on the bed.

I took a sip of coffee. "Well, I suppose we might as well clear some air. Find out what we're going to do and so on. Okay with the two of you?"

They nodded yes.

"First off, I'd like you both to know my main motive in coming down here is just what I told you last night, to fulfill my obligation to Oriana—that is, to find her murderer. But before we begin, I'd like to know why you, Margo, decided not to tell me your real name is Katheryn Marsden?"

Katheryn almost spilled her coffee.

Helen looked at me wide-eyed. "You *are* a Sherlock Holmes, aren't you? How did you figure that out?"

"Good coffee. Found a four-leaf clover."

"I don't understand." Katheryn looked bewildered. She apparently didn't know about her birthmark. No reason she should unless she was double-jointed or a mirror freak.

"If you're willing to assume an unladylike posture, Katheryn, I'll show you what I mean. Or you could go to the bathroom and have a private look at yourself."

Now, if there is one thing a naked dancer thinks she knows about, it's her body. What details she hasn't examined herself there's generally some nut in the audience willing to tell her. But the four-leaf clover bit had her bewildered.

"Listen, I bare my ass for horny old men almost every night. I haven't the foggiest idea what you're talking about." With that Katheryn disappeared inside her housecoat and apparently examined her anatomy with renewed interest.

"What do you see under there?" asked Helen.

"Not a damned thing. Same old stuff," came a muffled voice. Katheryn's head emerged from the top of her housecoat and her legs descended from the bottom. "Well, what is it you want me to do?"

"It might be a bit much." I rolled my tongue on the inside of my cheek.

"Oh, shit, what is it?"

"I want you to stand up, hike your housecoat up over your ass, spread your legs, and bend over."

Katheryn raised her eyebrows. Helen giggled.

"You're sure," said Katheryn. She put her cup of coffee on the floor.

"You wanted to know how I knew you were Katheryn Marsden. Maybe you don't want to know that much."

Katheryn didn't know if she wanted to expose herself all that much. "That's obscene," she said.

I shrugged my shoulders. "There's an easier way."

Katheryn had apparently decided to get it over with, in

much the same way a swimmer takes a dare to jump into an icy stream. She leaped off the chair, flipped the housecoat over her back with a flourish, and exposed her nether parts to Helen and me.

"See there, Helen," I said casually. "Four-leaf clover." I poked the birthmark with my finger.

The housecoat dropped abruptly. Helen giggled.

Katheryn turned around with an odd look on her face. "Come on now, you two. What's going on?"

"Get your little compact mirror, sweets, and see for yourself," said Helen.

Katheryn left for the bathroom and returned in a few minutes laughing as loud as Helen. "I never knew I had that. I never knew. A perfect four-leaf clover. How did you know?"

I told her Pete Lindbloom's story.

"My father knew? Why didn't he tell me? Why didn't my mother tell me? I could have had an Irish stage name at Bill's."

Helen shook her finger at me. "Oh, you naughty boy. I'll bet you were nosing around my buns last night looking for clover. Bet you snuck into the living room amd grabbed a quick look at poor Katheryn while she was sleeping."

"Nope. Spotted it when Margo passed her ass in review at the end of her dance. When we first entered Bill's Bawdies."

"I'll be damned," said Katheryn.

"Which brings me back to the question of why you didn't tell me your real name."

Neither of them said anything.

"I'll get us some more coffee," said Helen. She got up and got us refills while Katheryn and I sat in silence, me on the bed and she on the chair.

Helen sat down, took a sip of coffee, and looked me in the eyes. "We were afraid," she said.

"Afraid of what?" I had the feeling they still might be just a tad bit wary of me. "Afraid I might be the man who murdered Oriana Kauffmann?"

Helen nodded.

Helen looked at Katheryn and began to blink rapidly. "I'm afraid it's more than that."

I had suspected the night before that Katheryn had been crying. She broke down now into a dreadful, heartrending wailing.

I didn't know what to do except press on. "Since your parents are among the missing, I'm going to take a guess and say he might have murdered them also."

Katheryn couldn't answer. She was overcome by grief, anger, and bitterness at the gods, fate, fortune, bad luck, or whatever or whoever it was that had taken her parents from her.

Helen looked helplessly at her friend; her own eyes welled over with tears. She nodded yes. "Katheryn got a call; a man said he had murdered her parents. Just like that, he said it. Said it served her father right."

Katheryn was overwhelmed by wracking, spastic, awful crying. Both her parents were dead. Her parents and her good friend. I had an idea that Katheryn felt just a little responsible.

Helen got up from her chair and slipped under the sheets for a good bawl. She wanted back in the bed where it was warm and safe.

I took a guess. "This man, he said he wanted the manuscript or he would kill one of you?"

"Yes."

I was right. I tried again. "He picked Oriana."

Katheryn was too overcome to be of any help. Helen did the talking.

"We decided to give him the damned manuscript. We went to get it, but when we got back to the apartment, Oriana was gone. There was no note, nothing. Two days later we got a call from the same man. He said Katheryn was dead."

"He specifically said Katheryn, not Oriana?"

"Yes, Katheryn. I answered the phone and he said, 'Katheryn's dead.' I didn't correct him."

"Why not?"

"Because Katheryn knows almost as much about Shakespeare's manuscripts as her father. There are a lot of Shakespeare experts around, but she also knows her paper and her inks."

"You thought Oriana may have told him she was Katheryn, hoping he wouldn't kill her?"

Helen nodded yes. "Exactly. The seller still needs to prove the manuscript is real. The University of Texas has bucks okay, but it's damned well not gonna pay one and a half million dollars for a bogus play."

I thought that one over. Fast thinking, ladies, I granted them that. They were probably getting their kicks watching average wheels grind slowly in my transparent skull. "Wait a minute now. From what I see in the papers, nobody knows for sure if this play is the real thing or not."

Katheryn stopped her crying as suddenly as she had started and gave me one hell of a determined look.

"It's real."

"How do you know?"

"Because it's my business to know. In three months I'll have my Ph.D. in English literature from Berkeley. I've seen it; it's real. It's real and it will prove that Edward de Vere, Earl of Oxford, was really William Shakespeare. I assume you already know about a man named Sir Giles Twigg-Pritchart, the bastard."

"Only what I read in the papers."

"Isn't that enough!" She looked vehement.

"Why doesn't he make a grand announcement that it's bogus and let everyone wonder? The people at the University of Texas would howl, but they're Texans. Everybody knows about Texans."

Katheryn shook her head in disgust. "Computers," she said.

"What?"

"The University of Texas would simply program Shakespeare's vocabulary, grammar, syntax, and the rest of it through a computer and match the findings with *Jonathan Claiborne.* You can't bullshit a computer. Sir Giles knows that."

"So what do you want with me, besides finding Oriana's killer? Remember, that's why I came to San Francisco. *Riders of the Purple Sage* and all that."

"What?"

"If I hadn't pulled that jackass stunt in Zane Grey's drift, I would probably have gone on home to Seattle where I belong, drunk a little screw-top, thrown a few darts in Pig's Alley."

Helen had apparently been listening to my interrogation of Katheryn. She turned on her side in the bed, her face swollen from the crying. "After he murdered Oriana, we decided the son of a bitch can fuck himself. We're gonna sell *Jonathan Claiborne* to the University of Texas and get him in the process."

She sounded like she meant it.

I took a deep breath and let it out slowly. I figured right then that I must be the biggest sucker on the West Coast. "Did you receive any more threats?" I asked.

"The morning the papers had the stories about Oriana we got another call. The same man. He said he was going to be watching us. He said we should leave the manuscript in our unlocked apartment so he could pick it up at his leisure. He said if we didn't do that, he would kill another one of us."

"So that's why you brought Spectacles and Zapata along with you. You wanted protection in case I was a fraud."

Helen nodded yes.

"That's it," said Katheryn. "Will you help us?"

I looked her square in the eyes. "There are three people dead so far. If I join the game, my head's on the line too. Oriana or no, there are some questions I need answered before I go any further."

"Ask them," Helen said. I had a feeling they wanted to get everything out in the open. Catharsis time and all that.

"Number one, I guess, is something you might have volunteered on your own. Just how is it that a couple of naked dancers in San Francisco came by an unpublished manuscript by William Shakespeare that is wanted by a Peer of the Realm, the British Secret Service, the FBI, Harvard University, and the University of Texas, in addition to some jerk who runs around killing people? That's not to mention a student named Sayani whose property the play really is."

"My father," said Katheryn.

"I guessed that much. Where did he get the manuscript and how did you wind up with it?"

"A man who was trying to fence it to the University of Texas asked my father to verify its authenticity. The people at Texas apparently gave the owner a list of scholars qualified to make the examination and my father was at the top of the list. The man said he would give my father twenty-five hundred dollars to examine the manuscript and write a letter stating that it was real."

"The same man who later killed your parents and Oriana?"

"We think so."

"Now, what did your father do with the play after the man gave it to him?"

"It wasn't quite as easy as that. My father told him it

would take at least a week to do a competent analysis of the text plus study the paper and ink. He said he would have to have access to a computer to write a guarantee that would satisfy the regents of the University of Texas." At this point Katheryn took a deep breath.

I couldn't help but stare. Katheryn was apparently used to morons gaping at her. She continued with her story.

"The man said he would give my father two days. He said some Englishmen were following him, trying to steal the play. So he said my father would have to examine the manuscript in a motel room with him watching. My father said there was no way the University of Texas would pay one and a half million dollars for a manuscript examined in that manner. The man said it would have to do."

She paused, waiting for me to ask the inevitable.

"What did your father do?" I complied.

"He and my mother waited until the next morning when the man was in the bathroom shaving and they bolted. My father had written a note to me explaining all of it. He rushed the manuscript and the note into the nearest express mailbox."

"Oh, for Christ's sake. Why did he do that?"

"He didn't want to steal it, honest. He wanted to be the first man to give it a complete analysis, that's all. He planned on giving it back."

The more I was getting into this mess, the dumber it was becoming. The good professor was just a shade on the thick side if he thought he could borrow a manuscript worth $1.5 million with a cross-my-heart-hope-to-die promise to give it back.

"Why?" I asked.

"Promotion," said Katheryn.

"Promotion?"

"He had been stuck at associate professor for years. The administration said his list of publications was too short. The suggestion was that he had spent too much time feuding with Twigg-Pritchart and not enough time doing his homework. Six or eight days with that play would have given him a book and a dozen or so scholarly articles in the best publications. It meant promotion to full professor. It meant everything to him."

I hoped so. It had cost him his life.

"So you think he mailed you the manuscript to be safe and then tried to drive south to San Francisco to meet you. But the heavy caught up with him somewhere along the way."

"That's what I think." With that Katheryn hunkered over again and picked up her crying where she left off. Wracking shoulders, the whole bit.

I sat cross-legged on the bed for twenty minutes listening to her cry. On the other side of me Helen joined in the wailing every now and then but mostly controlled herself. I stared at the ceiling. When the waterworks subsided at last, I pressed on for what I had to know.

"Okay, now I want to know who those two guys were who escorted you to that tavern rendezvous, Helen."

"They're bouncers for Bill's Bawdies," said Helen.

"And part of the clientele at Dick's Ding Dong?"

Katheryn nodded.

"They don't know anything," said Helen. "Katheryn goes by Margo Kiner at Bill's. They know Oriana—she danced there too and lived here with us. We showed them the article in the papers and said we wanted to hire you to find Oriana's murderer."

I thought that one over. Spectacles and Zapata were young men with time on their hands. It was too much to expect they wouldn't be charmed by the idea of a million bucks. If the girls had the play, why shouldn't they lift as much as the next guy? "I guess there's no harm done there," I said.

"Now what?" said Helen.

"Now we settle the manuscript business. I came here to find Oriana's murderer. I told you that and I meant it. I don't want the play. I don't even want a third of the action. But if I fence *Jonathan Claiborne* with a killer on my ass, I think I deserve at least ten percent if I turn the trick. How's that?"

"Sounds fair to me," said Katheryn.

"Shall we shake on it or what?" Helen leered suggestively.

I rolled my eyes. "We'll shake on it. I don't have the energy for anything else."

Before we left I fished my Polaroid camera from the trunk of the Fiat. I took it up to the girls' apartment in a paper bag and, while they watched with some bewilderment, I put a quart jar of water in the bottom of the plastic trash pail in their kitchen to give it some weight. I put the trash back in and took a picture of it with my camera.

"Why are you doing that?" Helen asked.

"An offering to the gods," I said.

We hit the streets in search for someplace that still served breakfast. I saw Zapata standing on a street corner, looking interested in a crack on the sidewalk. Over eggs and hash browns I asked Katheryn why a candidate for the Ph.D. would want to spend her time dancing naked in a bar.

Katheryn brightened. "I was wondering when you were going to ask that. The answer should be pretty obvious."

"What's that?" Dumb John.

"You ever tried typing for a living?"

"No."

"Well, I have. It's terrible. The price is right on the ramp. All you have to do is get up there and move around."

There was just one more question. I asked it just as Katheryn stuffed a rasher of bacon in her mouth.

"Where is *Jonathan Claiborne* now?" I asked casually.

The bacon was inside the mouth, but the teeth didn't move. Katheryn looked at Helen.

"Might as well tell him," said Helen.

"We've got it in a locker at the Oakland bus station."

What could I do but laugh. "Been going to the movies again, I see. You should have mailed it to a pawnshop. Didn't Sam Spade mail the blackbird to a pawnshop?"

I shouldn't have said that. To say they were irritated would be putting it mildly. I spent the rest of my breakfast listening to the stoic chewing of hash browns. That and wondering what it was that I had missed.

CHAPTER 8

So there it was. If I was to find out who killed Oriana Kauffmann, then I'd have to play along with the risky business of fencing Shakespeare's play to the University of Texas. If I had had any class, I probably would have tried to get Katheryn and Helen to go with the lesser offer from Harvard. On the other hand, what the hell: They have genuine scholars in Texas. I couldn't imagine them using the manuscript as toilet paper. That's what Sir Giles Twigg-Pritchart had in mind.

After we finished breakfast, I lingered over my coffee and once again saw the girl's face there on the river. It was hard to imagine that I would ever forget her.

One thing that could have bothered me if I had let it was the fact that the manuscript didn't exactly belong to Katheryn and Helen. It's not that I felt it belonged to history, posterity, the British people, Sir Giles Twigg-Pritchart, the Modern Language Association, or all the little children of the future. No, it was the property of a Goan named

Sayani, who had inherited it as the legacy of his seagoing ancestors.

That didn't bother me for long. I looked across the table and locked onto Helen's eyes. I completely forgot about poor Sayani's misfortune.

When we got back to the apartment, I dug the paper out of the plastic trash barrel and there, taped to the top of the jar of water I had left on the bottom, was a note:

Dear Mr. Denson,

You Americans are usually so bloody stupid in these matters that it's not a whole lot of fun taking your goodies. You may think you're quicker, but we'll win in the end. Have a good time with the birds.

I showed the note to Katheryn. Her eyes widened. "Who's this?" she asked and passed it to Helen, who seemed equally bewildered.

"An Englishman," said Helen. "Bloody and birds."

"Either an Englishman or somebody who wants me to think he's English," I said. "We'll see."

"What do we do now?" asked Katheryn.

"We don't retrieve the manuscript and take the first plane to Austin. It's worth too much money to Oriana's murderer and too much ego to our friend Twiggy."

"That doesn't answer my question."

"We wait," I said.

"Wait?" said Helen.

"We wait until we know exactly who the players are. Then we'll know how to play the game."

We didn't have to wait long. When the girls picked up their mail a couple of hours later, there was an envelope addressed to me. Inside the letter there was a note and a

Polaroid snap of the top of the kitchen trash barrel.

I had to grin when I read the note:

Dear Mr. Denson,

The enclosed snap is off the top of the trash basket as we left it. Maybe we can share some information. Sir Giles would like to have a chat with you. Please have a seat in the lobby of the Alastair Hotel at 4 P.M. *We have chosen a nearby bar where we can drink some Guinness and maybe have a sandwich. Sir Giles likes a snack in the late afternoon. We understand you're fond of smoked salmon and raw cauliflower. We'll have some. Leave the birds at home."*

The top of the wastebasket was different in my picture. The British were giving me proof that someone had searched the girls' apartment after they left. Whoever it was must have snickered at the note taped to the top of the jar. But the British agent was one step ahead of him. The gentlemen of Her Majesty's Secret Service had much experience in these matters.

Helen and Katheryn didn't like the turn of events. They didn't want me to meet with Sir Giles.

"Why do you want to meet him?" Katheryn asked. "We already know he wants to destroy the manuscript. What's in it for us?"

"Better to know your opponent," I said.

"How do we know he won't beat our offer?"

I could feel both women watching me carefully.

"You don't," I said. "You'll have to trust me. I came down here looking for a murderer, not a bundle of cash."

"I still don't know," said Katheryn.

"I do," I said. "I'm going to take a nice civilized nap, then go have a beer with Sir Giles and his friends."

* * *

At 3 P.M. I got into my Fiat and took a leisurely drive to a parking garage some eight blocks from the Alastair. I had a half hour to kill, so I took my time walking the rest of the way. I cased the opposite side of the street using store windows as mirrors, and just two blocks from the hotel I spotted him, trying to look casual. Sheriff Philip Boylan had been watching too many James Bond movies. He carried a *Chronicle* under his arm, and each time I paused in front of a store the newspaper would unfold in front of his face. I felt like a circus trainer. Just see here, folks, all I have to do is pause in front of this window and the man across the street will unfold his newspaper. Watch him carefully now. See there. Remember, you saw it here first.

The bogus FBI agent named Andrew Carder was waiting for me in an overstuffed chair in the lobby of the Alastair. He rose with a warm smile and pumped my hand vigorously.

"I'm glad to see that you could make it."

"I don't think the girls were too happy about it," I said.

"I didn't think they would be, but what the hell!" He grinned. "By the way, did you spot your friend Sheriff Boylan out there?"

"He's got a real act with a newspaper, wouldn't you say?"

"He certainly does. I should think he would qualify for one of those amateur variety programs that are so popular on the telly over here." Carder looked wild-eyed and unfolded and folded an imaginary newspaper.

"I think Woody Allen would be good for the part," I said.

"Or Terry Thomas. I have a rear entrance cased. We can leave that way while our friend with the newspaper frets in the hot sun."

"Fine by me," I said. And I followed him.

Several blocks later Carder paused in front of a respectable old building that housed lawyers, stockbrokers, and other professionals. There was an unpretentious sign near the corner of the building that said DUKE's and nothing more. Duke's chose not to compete for the trashy set. Carder nodded his head. When I opened the door and stepped inside, he disappeared.

Duke's was dark and quiet if not exactly proper by an Englishman's standards. It was overpriced, but the young men in three-piece suits didn't seem to mind. They drank Heineken and chatted amicably about clients, accounts, and interest rates. The waitresses who served them moved quietly about the room clad in high-heel shoes, stylish net stockings, and stingy briefs. That's all. Judging from their apparent lack of interest, the young men found interest rates more fascinating than bare breasts.

I never could get used to a place like this. There is always a bit of the poor boy in me. On these occasions it shows. It makes me nervous paying two bucks for a bottle of Heineken when I can get a draft beer in a workingman's bar for sixty cents. There was that, plus the fact that I couldn't help staring. It's considered bad form to watch the passing breasts. A matter of status, I suppose. A classy guy will have seen a whole lot of bare breasts in his time. No need to gape. Not me. Not John Denson. I watch.

After my eyes adjusted to the darkness and the breasts, I saw there were two dart boards in one corner of the bar. A tall man with a thin face watched me from an isolated table.

I didn't have to be told.

That would be Sir Giles Twigg-Pritchart.

Anybody who had been involved in the intelligence community knew about Sir Giles. Meeting him was an extraordinary occasion and—in an odd sort of way—a privilege. He was a man who valued privacy, a fact that encourages myths and legends. He avoided cameras so few people knew what he looked like. Although he had two professions, two lives, he shunned public attention, referring to remain in the shadows. One part of Sir Giles Twigg-Pritchart was a professional spy dedicated to the old-school notion of intelligence as a game of wits among gentlemen. For more than thirty years he had designed elaborate schemes for agents of Her Majesty's Government around the world. He was said to be without equal in his ability to outwit Americans, Russians, French, Germans, Chinese, Japanese, Arabs, or anybody else foolish enough to take him on. In that role, Sir Giles was a faceless genius, storied bastard, and coldhearted son of a bitch. His other interest was William Shakespeare. A man of limitless ego, Professor Twigg-Pritchart fancied himself to be without equal in his knowledge of Shakespeare's work. And it was under cover of a Shakespearean scholar that he arranged appointments to Commonwealth universities around the world, there to live the good life among scholars and direct British intelligence operations in adjacent areas.

Sir Giles was about six feet four or five inches tall and weighed no more than 160 to 170 pounds. He was not old, no more than his early sixties. He had pale blue eyes, a proper moustache cut in the manner of Anthony Eden, and silver-gray hair. He wore a dark blue three-piece suit, the perfect model for Manhattan shirts or Beefeater gin.

He rose to his full height to meet me and shook my hand cordially.

I wondered if he remembered me as an obscure figure from his past.

He did. "I believe our paths have crossed before, Mr. Denson," he said politely.

"Yes, they have," I said. "Not under the most pleasant circumstances."

"Please, sit down. I'm glad that you could make it."

"Your man's note mentioned smoked salmon and raw cauliflower. How could I refuse?"

Sir Giles smiled. "Do you like Guinness? I understand

they have it here on draft. Gorgeous stuff on draft—pours like molasses."

"That would do just fine."

Sir Giles motioned over his head with his left hand and a waitress appeared with a tray of salmon and cauliflower plus a foaming pitcher of Guinness.

I couldn't help but notice that Sir Giles was a watcher too. "Had you told me about the waitresses, I'd have been even more eager," I said.

"They are lovely, aren't they?" Sir Giles poured the stout. He handed me my glass and watched me carefully. "Let's see, his name was Duncan something, wasn't it? A Scot as I recall."

"McDonald. An English plant at a classified IBM defense project at Owego, New York."

Sir Giles grinned. "Yes, that was it. McDonald. He had overextended himself, so he came home before he got the hook. Am I right?"

"You have a good memory."

"There's not much that I forget, Mr. Denson. Your people came after him. You, Mr. Denson, were assigned the hit."

I shrugged my shoulders. "Crapped in my mess kit."

"I never did understand how that happened."

"It's a long story. Just say I didn't really want to do it."

Sir Giles shook his head. "Destroyed your career. So now you're a sordid private detective chasing lost kids and interviewing people for lawsuits."

I shrugged my shoulders again and helped myself to some salmon and more Guinness.

"Say, whatever happened to that other young fellow, the one who finally made the hit on McDonald?"

"James Arnold. He was a friend of mine. He was murdered in bed six months later."

"I'm sorry to hear that," Sir Giles said. "Did they ever catch the killer?"

"No, they didn't, as you know."

Sir Giles tried some cauliflower. "It's a hard world, Mr. Denson. If only you people had given us an opportunity to debrief our man. He had the best stuff stashed away somewhere on microfilm and we never did get it."

"Well, I don't suppose you can win 'em all." I helped myself to some more stout. I was drinking too fast.

"I am a poor loser, Mr. Denson. Did I tell you that we've done a little homework on you?"

"I'd have been surprised if you hadn't," I said.

"They tell me you drink too much and have mixed luck with women."

"Both true," I said.

"They also tell me that you are very good at your work. I see we need more stout." He signaled for more and paused to pull at his nose.

"I don't imagine the service in your club back home is so charming," I said.

"No, Mr. Denson, indeed not." Sir Giles glanced casually at the breasts of the girl who arrived with another pitcher of Guinness. "I'm told, Mr. Denson, that it's possible to buy almost everything here in San Francisco."

"They are gorgeous, aren't they? Yes, I suppose it is."

Sir Giles smiled, ever the gentleman. "It's not just the girls I'm talking about. I know I can buy their services."

I helped myself to some salmon to give myself some time. "Marvelous salmon, Sir Giles. Sockeye, I believe. The very best."

"Thank you, Mr. Denson." Sir Giles started to say something else but I continued.

"You can't catch sockeye on a lure, you know. Only Chinook and silvers. The commercial people net the sockeyes."

Sir Giles was undaunted. "I would like to purchase the bogus Shakespeare, Mr. Denson."

"If I say no right now, will you take away the salmon and the stout?"

"Not at all, not at all. We British are civilized. I understand that some negotiations can be delicate."

A guy like Twigg-Pritchart doesn't talk about negotiations unless there's no other way around it. "So long as that's understood, you might as well say what's on your mind."

"I have a lot of money at my disposal, Mr. Denson. I am prepared to beat the offer made by your lady friends. And may I congratulate you on your taste in women. You must have a great deal of stamina."

I shrugged my shoulders and helped myself to some more stout. "What if the manuscript really is by William Shakespeare?"

"I suppose it's theoretically possible for it to be by William Shakespeare, but it is inconceivable for it to be by Edward de Vere. I don't propose to argue the matter of authorship. If the manuscript is destroyed, there is no argument."

"I guess I still don't understand."

" 'Good name in man and woman, dear my lord,
'Is the immediate jewel of their souls;
'Who steals my purse steals trash; 'tis something, nothing;
' 'Twas mine, 'tis his, and has been slave to thousands;
'But he that filches from me my good name
'Robs me of that which not enriches him,
'And makes me poor indeed.' "

It was obvious I was supposed to recognize the quote. I didn't and it showed.

Sir Giles looked disappointed. "A matter of your American education, I suppose, eh, Mr. Denson?"

I didn't say anything. I played his game. "You're right, of course. I do know the part about the witches in *Macbeth.*

'Double, double toil and trouble;/Fire burn and cauldron bubble.' All that. Read it in the eighth grade."

"My quote was from *Othello*, Mr. Denson."

"I've been in Othello. Went hunting mule deer there when I was a kid. Great big bastards, hang out in the rimrocks."

Sir Giles looked displeased.

"That's in eastern Washington," I said. "Not much happening there most of the time." Sir Giles did not joke about William Shakespeare.

"Mr. Denson, if you don't sell us what we want, we will take it from you."

"Does your British side make a habit of playing on the American pitch?"

"Ahh, a football fan, are you?"

I shrugged my shoulders.

"Your players would not make our second division, you know that. You buy over-the-hill stars like George Best, but you still can't play football."

I helped myself to more Guinness and more salmon. "You didn't answer my question," I said.

"I should have thought the fate of your friend James Arnold would answer that. Tell me, did you ever have the opportunity to see George Best in his prime?"

I shook my head no.

"He had a dozen moves at once going on goal. The man marking him wouldn't know what to do. Just when he least expected, George would fire it past at the nets. The keeper never stood a chance."

"Are you telling me I'm up against a George Best in his prime?"

"No, Mr. Denson. When I was younger I fancied myself a cricket player. I know football is supposed to be a working-man's game, but I like it as well. I like the crowds."

"You are telling me you have a lot of moves."

"I am that. More than you'll ever mark."

"How many of you are there? Just you and Mr. Carder?"

Sir Giles shook his head. "I'm surprised at you. Of course not. Even George Best needed help getting through the defenders. I let you see Andrew today because you figured him out in Roseburg. Incidentally, that was a very nice piece of thinking. My congratulations."

"Listen, I thought you were retired from the business. I don't understand what this is all about."

"Of course you do, Mr. Denson. You may be a bit reckless and rough on the edges, but you're not slow. Our sources are confident on the latter point. I was about to be retired to Oxford had it not been for an outrageous academic named Marsden. He queered the deal. Is that how you Americans would phrase it?"

"That's one way," I admitted. "Then you're not going to all this trouble because of William Shakespeare's reputation?"

Sir Giles looked disappointed. "For heaven's sake, no. Oh, I suppose that has something to do with it. I put up with Anston Marsden's bellicose challenges for twenty years. I couldn't do much about him because my status as a professor was a cover. I'm a first-rate Shakespearean scholar, but I've also had other things on my mind, as you know. I haven't had the leisure to spend all my time tinkering with computers, which is the fashion in American universities. But this Marsden fellow, he just wouldn't bugger off. Have you read about the incident on the BBC last October?"

I shook my head no. I wanted to hear his version. "I've heard about it, that's all. I don't know the details."

Sir Giles had a bit of stout himself and tried some salmon before he continued. "I tried to ignore it. Figured he was insecure, a man from the soil who was out of his limits, trying to prove he was a gentleman and not a philistine. All that. But he just wouldn't stop. The topper, as I said, came on a BBC panel discussion on Mr. Sayani's find. It was one of those awful affairs where the bloody viewers were supposed to ring in questions. Are you with me?"

"I'm with you," I said.

"The discussion was chaired by an ignorant journalist. In the middle of the damned thing, Marsden got heated. He called me a dilettante and a fraud and informed all of Great Britain that I was really an intelligence officer plying my dirty trade in the most prestigious Commonwealth universities around the world." The very thought of Marsden caused Sir Giles to take his frustration out on the enamel of his teeth. "Of course the people at Oxford knew about me; after all, Her Majesty's Government proposed to pay my salary for the remainder of my academic appointment. It was intended to be my reward, Mr. Denson, for distinguished service to Queen and Country. I had a good ten years left. But I was too tired for the spy business and knew it."

Sir Giles sighed and we fell silent.

"What happened then?" I asked at last.

"The people at Oxford couldn't go through with the deal. They were apologetic, of course, but they have their reputations, after all. I don't suppose they can be blamed."

I cleared my throat. "Did you murder Marsden and his wife?"

Sir Giles shrugged. "Your friend Arnold cost us our man on our turf."

"But what about Marsden and his wife?"

"If I did have them hit, I wouldn't admit it. If I didn't, it might not hurt for you to think I did. Does that make sense?" he smiled.

"I would have been surprised at any other answer. The FBI is in on this game as well. You know that."

"*Were* in on the game, Mr. Denson. It was an FBI agent who was in the girls' apartment after us this morning. However, not more than an hour ago I had a chat with the special agent in charge of the San Francisco field office. You people operate on our turf all the time. We don't get in your way unless our interest is directly involved. If someone lifted your Declaration of Independence and spirited it off to London, we wouldn't trail around after your people like a herd of cattle. That would be uncivilized and bad public relations as well. Shakespeare was an Englishman. The opinion of the herd is everything in a democracy."

What he said was true. Sir Giles Twigg-Pritchart could dispatch me with the FBI peering over his shoulder and nothing would be done about it. Since Americans don't have titles, they are awed by them. Sir Giles knew the correct way to eat soup. The government would not want to get involved in a scandalous affair with our British allies. It would be ugly. What would be the point? Where was the percentage?

"Bad PR is the very worst," I said.

"Exactly, Mr. Denson. Incidentally, two homosexual gentlemen spent the night in the shadow of the girls' apartment looking like caricatures of conniving Bolsheviks. I'm sure they smell money. I've taken steps to dissuade them. They won't be bothering you."

"That was kind of you," I said. "What about Sheriff Boylan?"

"What about him, Mr. Denson?"

"Will you be taking steps to dissuade him?"

"No, I don't believe so. I find him charming in a coarse and vulgar sort of way. Besides, I might have a use for him."

If Twigg-Pritchart kept Boylan around as a fool, there had to be a reason. A good reason. Sir Giles was a man who calculated every decision. He knew I was wondering why.

"Anything more, Mr. Denson?"

"Yes. Why are you dealing with me?"

Sir Giles didn't answer the question. "You know, we

didn't have much time in one day to find out about you, Mr. Denson. We do have some contacts in Seattle, however, so we rang them."

"That's where you found out about the cauliflower and the rest."

Sir Giles grinned. "Yes, that's where, as a matter of fact. Did you happen to notice the dart boards when you came in?"

"Why, yes, I did." I grinned right back. Sir Giles was a competitor. I could see his challenge coming.

"You throw in some sort of pub, we're told."

"Pig's Alley. It's a tavern that has jazz and dart boards. You can buy an Olympia or Rainier for a buck a bottle."

"I was under the impression that darts is a British game, better suited to our temperament." Sir Giles paused. "Like secret agents and all that."

I decided to let the second part pass. "A lot of people in Seattle throw darts these days."

"Do you think you're very good, Mr. Denson?"

"At darts?"

"Yes."

"I do okay, I suppose. How about yourself?"

"We had a board in the faculty club at the University of Singapore. Would you care to take me on in a game?"

"Sure, but those boards over there look hardly used. Do they have bar darts here?"

"Indeed."

The bar darts were light, about eighteen grams. I was used to twenty-three, but Sir Giles was probably used to heavier darts too. We each threw some warm-ups. Sir Giles stood confidently at the line. He knew how to throw.

"Shall we middle for the diddle, Mr. Denson? You may go first, if you like."

We threw. I was closest to the bull and would start the game. "Double on or straight on?" I asked.

Sir Giles smiled. "Why, double on, of course. That's the way the game is meant to be played. You play against me, Mr. Denson, and you play by the hardest rules."

Well, okay. Whatever. Sometimes I'm on. Sometimes I'm off. This time I was on. I hit the double fourteen the first throw and took Sir Giles out in twelve lovely darts. Not bad.

"The darts are light," he said.

"For both of us, Sir Giles."

"You're a diverting man, Mr. Denson. You know about football, which is surprising. You throw nice darts as well. But I mentioned another British game, I believe."

"Secret agents and all that."

"Yes. You might beat me with light darts, Mr. Denson, but I will get that bogus play. I have people with me."

I shrugged my shoulders. I suspected the reason why he wanted me with the girls was that I was a professional. He could anticipate a professional. But women? How could he know for sure?

The business with Boylan was another matter. That really was curious. Of what use could Boylan possibly be? What leverage would Twigg-Pritchart have?

Knowledge that Boylan was a murderer, that was one possibility.

Andrew Carder suddenly appeared from the shadows.

"Fine, fine," said Sir Giles. "I think our interview is finished now. Andrew, would you be so kind as to arrange for the services of the blonde with the extraordinary front? She looks a lot like the one in Cape Town, don't you think? If she isn't for hire, I would like one equally as charming."

Carder escorted me to the door.

"Helluva guy," I said. "Class."

"A real gentleman," Carder said.

I stepped out in the sun and Carder followed me. He knew I wanted a private word with him.

"Tell me," I said, "what do you think of our friend Boylan?"

Carder ran his tongue over his teeth and thought about that for a bit before he answered. "The way we understand it, Sayani told his professor about losing the play at lunch the day after it happened. The professor, a guy named Piper, got up and phoned the police and some chaps on the newspapers. You want to take it from there?"

"Sure," I said. "If he called before one P.M., he would have made the deadlines for the street finals of the afternoon paper. That sells mostly to tourists in Waikiki. Boylan would have been out chasing tail, just right to buy a paper off the rack and discover what it really was that he had found in his room. Right so far?"

"The way we see it," said Carder.

"The Honolulu police, being what all big-city cops are, took their sweet time. After all, there were no dead people involved, and what's Shakespeare to them? They watch television."

"And when the bloody sods finally did interview Boylan, they took his word for everything, him being a sheriff and all." Carder shook his head.

"So you think the girls have the manuscript?"

Carder smirked. "We know they do."

"All the lousy luck in the world!" I offered him my hand.

We shook on it.

"Same to you, friend," he said.

I drove to the federal building in San Francisco and parked in an overpriced lot. The bureaucrats had treated themselves to a building with a handsome stone facade at the entrance, soft carpets inside, with glass all around. There was soft music for those in the trying business of spending other people's money.

The San Francisco field office of the FBI was on the

sixth floor. The secretary was an efficient-looking woman in her late thirties.

"May I help you?"

"Yes, I would like to speak to the special agent in charge."

"That would be Mr. Montgomery. I'm afraid that would be impossible if you don't have an appointment."

Mr. Montgomery was probably staring at the street. Turning people down makes secretaries feel important; bosses with status casually refuse to see people. The status rubs off on the secretary. When I was a reporter, I was convinced there was an international conspiracy of efficient-looking secretaries. They were after me.

"Would you please tell Mr. Montgomery that I'm here to see him about British spies and a poet named Shakespeare."

"I'm afraid that would be impossible," she said automatically.

"If you don't, there may be an international incident and it'll be your ass, lady," I said just as automatically.

I don't think she liked me very much. She got up and disappeared through a door. She was out again ten seconds later.

"Mr. Montgomery will see you now," she said as though nothing had happened.

"Does he have a first name?"

"Mr. Montgomery's first name is Richard."

"Dick Montgomery. I bet he goes to the toilet," I said. I went into the office expecting to meet an officious jerk.

Montgomery was giggling like a fool. "I don't know what you said to her, Mac, but old Ethel out there was so wired she forgot to tell me your name."

"John Denson."

That made him giggle even louder. "The man with the human surfboard."

I even had to laugh at that one, although the whole

thing was beginning to wear. "Listen, I'm down here to—"

Montgomery cut me short. "I know. I know. You're part of a parade. Everybody's here to find a missing play by the bard of Avon. You want it. The British government wants it. A lot of screwball professors want it."

"Did Sir Giles Twigg-Pritchart turn you folks from the chase?"

"Well, I guess that's one way of putting it. Old Twiggy leaned on his friends in the British Foreign Office who leaned on the director. The director leaned on me. Me, I don't give a damn one way or the other, less forms to fill out."

"That tells me what I want to know there." I scratched my head as though questions didn't come easily. "How about Sheriff Philip Boylan?"

Montgomery massaged his temples with his left hand and shook his head. "That dumb shit! Beats the hell out of us. You know he was the guy who checked into that Waikiki hotel a few minutes after the kid with the play got mugged. Common sense tells you he wound up with it. What did he do with it then? He requested a mail hold on a girl named Katheryn Marsden as part of a murder investigation."

"The post office holding?"

"They're holding."

"Anything yet?"

Montgomery shrugged. "It's his investigation. Not our mail."

I knew better and gave him a look that said so.

He giggled. "Oh, we've taken a little peek, all right."

"And?"

"Nothing."

I started to go, but there was something that bothered me. "Listen, what will the FBI do with you when they find out you have a sense of humor?"

Montgomery looked surprised. "Why, they'll fire me, of course." He thought that was funny too.

CHAPTER

I took my time walking back to the parking lot. Boylan could have murdered both the Marsdens and the girl on the river; there was no doubt of that. On the other hand, it could just as easily have been Sir Giles and his crew. It wouldn't have taken long for the British to conclude that Boylan had found the manuscript in his hotel room and had taken it home to Roseburg with him. It would have been an easy matter for Carder and his mates to trail Boylan to Eugene if that's how the manuscript got to Katheryn's father.

Now what if, just what if, I asked myself, they got their paws on Marsden *after* he mailed his manuscript to his daughter but *before* he got very far down the pike. The British too can be persuasive interrogators.

Sir Giles was a man of immense ego. It wouldn't be enough for him merely to take his revenge on Marsden's hide. No, he would want everything—that included the missing play. He was a thorough man; he wouldn't want Marsden's ghost to haunt him from scholarly journals.

Just as bad would be to have Marsden's daughter do the job in his stead. To be undone by a young woman would be the final blow.

Now then, what would be Sir Giles's first instinct upon learning that Marsden had mailed the manuscript to his daughter?

He would try to intercept it.

But he obviously hadn't, and that was curious.

I didn't pay any attention to Boylan, who was watching the parking lot from an old Buick parked in a truck loading zone across the street. I dropped by a grocery store to pick up a half gallon of screw-top before I returned to the girls' apartment building. A slender brunet was sitting in the plastic chair by the soda machine reading a two-year-old copy of *Time* magazine when I punched the Up button.

I punched and the girl put her magazine down and stood up.

"Mr. Denson?"

"Yes."

She had a copy of the *Chronicle* folded under her arm and I guessed my picture was somewhere on the inside. "Mr. Denson, my name is Katheryn Marsden and I would like a word with you—in private if that's possible."

My mouth must have dropped five feet. "Lady, life has its surprises, but it would be surprising indeed if your name is Katheryn Marsden."

"Would you like to see my identification?" She had a pleasant smile.

She also had a pleasant figure. More than pleasant. I was thinking, hell, yes, lady, I'd like nothing better than to have a look at your ID. "Sure," I said.

She handed me a wallet from her handbag. "Have a look," she said.

I looked. California's driver's license. Social security card. A card with her picture on it identifying her as a graduate student at the University of California, Berkeley. A card identifying her as an associate member of the Modern Language Association. It was all there. The works. With pictures.

The elevator arrived and the door opened.

"Mr. Denson, the girl up there who claims to be Katheryn Marsden is an imposter. Please believe me. I rented her my apartment for the summer because I planned on being away."

Oh, shit, I thought, one damned thing after another. "Can you explain exactly how that is in twenty-five words or less, or will it take longer?"

"Longer, I'm afraid." She seemed genuinely concerned at causing me to have to go out of my way. Her brown eyes watched me and blinked.

"I suppose it would be too much to hope that you're not in the market for Shakespeare's lost play?"

"Yes, it would, Mr. Denson. I have every reason to believe my father gave his life for that manuscript."

Oh, for Christ's sake. Fathers and daughters. "Listen, I've been drinking stout this afternoon with a British intelligence officer but . . ."

"Sir Giles Twigg-Pritchart," she interrupted.

". . . but I don't suppose it would hurt to have a few more. If you wouldn't mind accompanying me to the nearest bar."

"Not at all, Mr. Denson. We have a family friend in the Seattle police department. His name is Donald Gilmore and I called him after I read about you in the newspapers. He said you are the genuine article, as he put it, and can be trusted."

I knew Don Gilmore was okay, but I was thinking about four-leaf clovers just then and was confused as hell.

So I loaded the Great Pretender into my Fiat and, accompanied as usual by the fanatical Boylan, found a comfortable bar. This one was called Bob's, nothing more, and did not feature velvet penises, naked ladies, jukeboxes, video games, or anything else. Just booze and quiet.

I ordered a pitcher of Coors and two glasses and we settled down on either side of a booth to talk. I must have made a poor impression on Sir Giles for him to think I could be had this easily. On the other hand, I was curious as to what the girl's pitch would be.

She led with a fastball.

"I have an idea, Mr. Denson, that the girl upstairs who claims to be me is a plant by Sir Giles Twigg-Pritchart. Did you check her identification carefully?"

"Sort of," I said. "Can you tell me where you have been and, if she is an impostor, how she was able to pull it off?"

She smiled at that and took a moderate sip of beer. I got the impression that she was not a beer drinker. "Do you know what the PEN is, Mr. Denson?"

Indeed I did. A serious international organization of writers and scholars. I nodded yes.

"I'm not a member of PEN; that is an honor reserved for an elite of published authors. I am employed as a secretary for that organization, a position secured for me by my father, who is a member. PEN has been holding its annual convention this past week in Tokyo. That's where I have been. My landlord went on vacation two days after I left. His niece took his place. We've never met."

"You think those girls up there have hired me to help sell your mail?" I took in a lungful of air and let it out slowly. Not a bad effect.

"That's exactly what I think, Mr. Denson. It isn't right. I know that and you know that."

I had to admit she sounded more like a scholarly broad should sound like, but you never could be sure. Besides which, there were too many things that didn't add up. What the hell, I decided to try anyway.

Ms. Marsden, if that's who she was, was fine looking. And she seemed so damned honest it was hard not to believe her.

I tried to look a bit thick, which was fairly easy to do. "Listen, would you run through that again?"

"I don't know what those girls up there told you, but they're my tenants. I planned on being in London and Tokyo for the summer and I leased them my apartment. They were supposed to forward my mail to me. But I think Sir Giles paid them to steal the manuscript for him."

I whistled. "That's quite a lot to expect of two girls who dance in the raw."

Katheryn II ignored my interruption. "But I also think the idea of one and a half million dollars was too much to pass up, so they decided to con you into slipping it past him to the University of Texas."

"Me?"

"You. I told you Donald Gilmore said you were 'the genuine article.' What I didn't add was the very idea of you being mixed up in this business struck him as being outlandishly funny."

She couldn't suppress a grin. Christ, she was cute.

"A real belly buster," I said. If this lady was a fake, Sir Giles had done a helluva job so far. But there was no turning back now. I had to go all the way. "How far would you go to prove you're Katheryn Marsden?"

"How far do you have to go? I've given you all the identification you could possibly need."

"All of which could be faked."

Katheryn II took that very seriously. "Just what is it that would satisfy you, Mr. Denson?"

"I have a question to ask and I don't want to come off sounding like a pervert."

"What is it?"

"Miss Marsden, would you be willing to drop trou for a, uh, personal inspection?"

"Drop trou?"

"Trousers. Drop your trousers."

Katheryn II leaped up from her seat and bolted from Bob's quiet bar.

Hoo, boy, had I ever played that one wrong!

There were two possibilities. She was either the real Katheryn and didn't know about her little clover or she was Sir Giles's plant and did the only thing she could. This was no time to piss and moan.

I followed her.

She was wearing a tight skirt and her buns moved like two squirrels in a plastic bag as she hustled down the hot sidewalk. "You stay away from me," she shouted back over her shoulder. Her feet went *tap, tap, tap*. So sweet!

What a fine ass! "Listen," I shouted. "The real Katheryn Marsden has a dark red birthmark in the shape of a four-leaf clover on the inside of her left buttock. I have that on authority of one Dr. P. D. Lindbloom who delivered her in Roseburg, Oregon."

Katheryn II stopped dead in her tracks. That's a cliché, I know, but it's the only way to describe how fast she stopped.

"Is that the truth?"

"That's what Pete said."

"How come I never knew about it?"

"Your father thought it would embarrass you."

She thought that one over. "You come with me to my hotel room and we'll see."

The very idea caused a stirring in my loins, as the euphemism goes.

She had a proper suite in a proper hotel.

Once we were inside, she motioned for me to have a seat on her living-room sofa.

"I suppose I'll have to examine myself in the bathroom," she said. She gave me what I must describe as a level look and disappeared.

"You'll have to use a mirror," I called after her. "Careful not to fall off the sink."

She didn't answer.

I waited.

She was laughing when she returned. The same reaction as Katheryn I. "You're right. There is a clover there. I never knew that. I never knew that."

"Mind if I have a look?"

"Of course I mind if you have a look. Who do you think you are?"

"Listen, I'm not gonna try to lay you. But seeing's believing. If you want me to help you out, you're gonna have to drop your pants. There's just no other way."

"No other way?"

"None."

Katheryn II turned around, hiked her skirt up, pulled her pants down, and with the index finger of her left hand pulled one buttock out.

There it was.

Jesus Christ!

Right where it was supposed to be.

She pulled her pants back up and dropped her skirt. "Now do you believe me?"

"Miss Marsden, I'll be frank; I don't know what to believe." I was finding it hard to forget that fine little bun being pulled to one side.

"Please, call me Katheryn."

"I'll tell you what, I'll do the best I can. I can't promise anything. The smartest thing I can do is go back there like nothing happened and play along with their game. See if there's anything I can do. What do you say?"

"Sounds fair to me. You can call me here at the Palisades Hotel if you need anything."

"I'll do that."

I stood up to leave.

"One more thing, Katheryn."

"What's that?"

"I think you have a perfectly marvelous tush."

She blushed. It had been a long time since I'd seen someone do that.

"Why, thank you. I think you'd better be going now."

I went.

I went back to my Fiat, where I sat on the front seat, watched the traffic, and thought. My problem was fairly clear. Sir Giles preferred soccer metaphors. I liked fishing ones better.

Only one of the two Katheryns was real. On the one hand, I had a Katheryn Marsden who lived her life as Margo Kiner, nude dancer. On the other, I had Katheryn II. You'd think that a birthmark in the shape of a four-leaf clover on the inside of the left buttock would be enough to identify any woman in the world.

Not this time.

One of the Katheryns was real and the other was a plant by Sir Giles Twigg-Pritchart. Maybe. Or they could both be fakes.

If Katheryn I was the plant, she was dumb enough to think she could outwit Sir Giles.

I could just see Sir Giles with an arrogant smirk on his face. A helluva story for his retirement. Yes, sir, a naked dancer. You couldn't get any wilder than that. I don't imagine he had ever gone after steelies. But a steelhead lure she was—too flashy to be real but too provocative to ignore.

The lure, the water, everything was just right. Only in this case it appeared Sir Giles might have hooked himself in the butt on his foreswing. The reason was that Katheryn-

Margo and her pal Helen could read newspapers. The newspapers told them virtually everything they needed to know.

And $1.5 million was a lot of money, a whole lot more than Sir Giles was paying. It was possible, just possible, that they double-crossed him, provided Margo with a cosmetic clover, and picked a gullible sap like me to fence their property.

No damn fun at all.

The other possibility was that Katheryn I really was Katheryn Marsden and the wholesome girl who stepped out of central casting was the plant, a trout fly sent forth by Sir Giles to con me into screwing Katheryn out of her play.

Whatever his other shortcomings, Twigg-Pritchart must have a fun sense of humor. I like to laugh too, but I still had two unanswered questions: Who was the dead girl on the river and who murdered her?

I had thought she was Oriana Kauffmann; now I wasn't so sure.

CHAPTER 10

I pulled over in front of a phone booth a mile from the girls' apartment.

The first thing I did was call my answering service. Emma took the call in that special voice of hers; I felt a pang of regret that I had such harsh feelings about Kahlil Gibran. I had once considered an attempted brainwash of Emma, maybe introduce her to Raymond Chandler or somebody, but thought better of it.

"Oh, Mr. Denson, it's so good to hear from you. We've all been wondering if you're safe and everything," she said. It was nice to be missed.

Might be worth it after all, I thought. "I'm just fine, Emma. Just checking on the calls."

"Well, Mr. Denson, we have a lot of repeats. Mr. Steinberg, the agent. Mr. Diamond, the ghostwriter. Mr. Diamond says he's been reading about Professor Marsden, Sir Giles Twigg-Something, and the Shakespeare play and says your story's even better than he thought at first. I also got calls again from Mr. Swinn, the ABC television man, and from

Professor Piper, who says he is in San Francisco and is very anxious to meet you."

"Professor Piper?"

"Yes, Mr. Denson. That's Nicholas Piper."

"Go on."

"You got a call from a Mrs. Wilma Anderson who lives here in Seattle. Mrs. Anderson's daughter apparently ran off with a fundamentalist religious cult that lives communally. Mrs. Anderson wants you to find her daughter. She said you were recommended by Sergeant Holcomb of the Seattle police department."

"Did you tell her I'll call back?" The Wilma Andersons of the world paid my rent.

"You also got a call from a man named George Browning. Mr. Browning said he is an insurance broker and that his wife, Alicia, has been having an affair with a hairdresser. He said a shyster in town said you could take the 'necessary pictures.'"

The George Brownings also paid my rent. "Did you get his number, Emma?"

"I sure did, Mr. Denson. Mr. Denson?"

"Yes, Emma."

"Mr. Denson, Mr. Browning said the hairdresser was a fag. Do you really think the hairdresser would be having an affair with his wife if he was a homosexual?"

"I doubt that, Emma. But you never know, I guess. It takes all kinds."

Emma cleared her throat on the other end. That was her signal that she was embarrassed. She was sexy even when she cleared her throat. "Mr. Denson, we girls here were wondering what Mr. Browning meant by 'necessary pictures.'"

"Just what you girls think, Emma. He wants them so he won't have to pay alimony or maybe can get custody of the kids if he wants them."

Emma giggled. "Do you really take those kind of pictures, Mr. Denson?"

"Certainly. The United States government taught me how to take them. I've got a collection of real fun prints in my apartment."

"Mr. Denson!" Emma tried to sound shocked, but it didn't come off.

Maybe she was ready to be weaned from Kahlil Gibran after all. I got the numbers of Wilma Anderson, George Browning, Nicholas Piper, and hung up. I couldn't afford to keep paying clients waiting forever. I had to make a move.

I decided to take a flyer on Professor Nicholas Piper. I gave him a call.

"Oh, hello," said the man who answered. He sounded like I had roused him from a nap.

"I'd like to speak to Professor Nicholas Piper, please."

"That's I."

"Professor Piper, my name is John Denson."

"Glad that you called. I've been trying to get in touch with you, Mr. Denson. And please call me Nick."

"Well, Nick, I've never met you, so I'm taking a bit of a chance here. I think we may be able to do business, but first I have to assure myself that you are who you say you are. Does that make sense?"

"Of course. I have no objections. But how do you propose to do that?"

"My fear is that you might be a British agent. You're a professor of American studies, is that right?"

"That's right."

"The British, like all modern intelligence organizations, have the dossiers of all their agents fed into a computer so if they want an expert on American culture, all they have to do is punch him up. You follow me?"

"That makes sense."

"But the odds are against them having a man in their banks who is both an American studies man and who knows Honolulu. You still follow?"

"I follow."

"So I want to ask you some questions—some serious, some frivolous, just like in the spy movies."

"I'll do my best," said Piper.

I took a deep breath and thought about it a moment before proceeding.

"Who was it, Nick, who coined the phrase, 'The only good Indian is a dead Indian'?"

"Phil Sheridan," he said without a pause.

Not bad. "Exactly," I said. "Who was Horace Greeley's European correspondent?"

"Karl Marx. That one was too easy. Any schoolboy worth his salt knows that."

"What was James Madison's school?" Too easy also.

"Princeton." He was laughing on the other end.

"Okay. Who first used the assembly line in this country?"

"It wasn't Henry Ford. Nobody knows for sure. One nice guess is hog slaughtering in Cincinnati, 1836."

I thought it was Ford, but I kept my mouth shut. "Acceleration of history?"

"Henry Adams."

He was good. I was damned near out of useless bits of information.

"What was Queequeg's profession?"

"Harpoonist."

That wasn't good either. I decided to try a couple about Hawaii.

"What is an *okole*?"

"One's behind."

"How about *kuleana*?"

"One's area of expertise."

"*Puka?*"

"Hole, Mr. Denson." Piper was really laughing now.

"Used in what context?"

"In virtually any context you might care to imagine."

I had to give up. "I tell you what, Nick, I quit."

"Did I pass?" I heard a tinkling of ice. He was having himself a drink.

"Good enough for the girls I go with."

"One question for you, Mr. Denson."

"What's that?"

"Who was the constable in *The Moonstone?*"

I knew the answer to that; I could hardly believe it. "Sergeant Cuff."

"Fair enough." Piper laughed. "You pass too."

"What I want to know now is why you're here, Nick. What is it you expected to get?"

The tinkle of ice again. "Mohan Sayani is a decent young man. I don't like to see him taken like this. I'd like to see him get enough money to take care of his education and maybe set him up as a solicitor in India. I'd like to see the play wind up in the Smithsonian Institution or the British Museum, but I know they don't have the money to outbid the University of Texas." More ice. "I want to help out."

"Is there anything about that manuscript that I should know about now?"

"Are you going by wire-service accounts or have you read the stories in the Sunday *Times?*"

"Mostly wire service," I said. No need to tell him more.

The ice tinkled again. "Well then, you'll want to know the full details. Copies of a manuscript in the author's own hand are known as foul copies. Copies prepared by a professional scribe are known as fair copies. A fair copy in Tudor times had to be approved by a censor before it could be printed. Earlier in the sixteenth century that was done by the Stationers' Company, but by the time most of Shakespeare's plays were recorded, that task was done by a court official known as the Master of Revels. Are you with me?"

"So far," I said.

"In addition to foul and fair copies, there were prompter's copies as well. A prompter's copy simply had stage directions added. And then we have the quartos, those plays actually set into type and printed. There are bad quartos, those plays pirated from rival productions or stolen from competing theaters and published in bastard form. And there are accurate quartos, called, sensibly enough, good quartos. The Shakespeare from Stratford-upon-Avon died in 1616. Beginning in that year two men named John Heminges and Henry Condell began work on a folio of Shakespeare's complete works. Their effort, which has become the standard reference, was completed in 1623."

"What does all this have to do with Sayani's find?"

"Well, the greater part of the manuscript is apparently a fair copy. That in itself is rare enough. I'm not certain there are extant fair copies. One thing I do know, and that is that there are no surviving foul copies, manuscripts in Shakespeare's own hand. Now apparently Shakespeare, or De Vere, had second thoughts about *Jonathan Claiborne*. Sayani said there was a one-page note on top of the manuscript giving instructions for certain changes in the play before it was sent to the Master of Revels. Those instructions, in the author's own hand, qualify as a foul copy and make the property even more valuable."

I could hear the ice tinkling again on Piper's end as I asked, "Does the fact that the play was found in De Vere's trunk prove he wrote it?"

"It's damned good circumstantial evidence, and combined with everything else it would make a tough argument."

"What if they compared the handwriting on that one-page foul copy with foul copy of De Vere's early poems?"

Piper laughed on the other end. "That would lock it up, wouldn't it?"

Indeed it would. Piper had given me everything I needed to know.

There, over the telephone, I told Piper the whole story. He didn't say anything for some time after I finished. I still could hear the ice.

"That's quite a story," he said at last. "I'm not sure, but I think I'm in over my head."

"I know damn well I am," I said. "What do you have there?"

"Martini on the rocks. Got a bottle of gin and a bucket of ice. What do you think?"

"About the gin or your proposition?"

"My proposition." Tinkling.

"If Katheryn and Helen told me the truth, we still have an agreement. If they're Katheryn Marsden's tenants or hastily recruited amateurs who double-crossed Twigg-Pritchart, then I don't know. I do know I can't do the job alone. I'm outnumbered by British professionals. If you do help and we succeed, then I guarantee you a fair shake."

I could hear Piper digging into his ice bucket. "What would be my share in the first instance, if the girls are telling the truth?"

I thought about that. What the hell? "Twenty-five thousand dollars for me, the same for you."

"And in the second case?"

"I'm not sure. That's up to the buyers. But you should understand before you agree to anything that we're up against people who don't fool around. They know what they're doing."

Piper cleared his throat. "Strikes me that you know what you're doing as well."

"Listen, if I had good sense, I wouldn't agree to a proposition like this in the first place. However, this is one time I think I could use a professor's help. Tell me, do you know anybody over at Berkeley?"

Piper laughed. "Lots of people. I was a visiting professor of American literature there three years ago."

I took a deep breath.

"Shakespearean scholars. Do you know any Shakespearean scholars?"

"I played tennis with Levi Goldman. He has a weak backhand and I would have beaten him except that my knees gave out. Too much weight. We had dinner a couple of nights ago. Levi's interested in this business and will help me out any way he can."

"Okay, Nick, here's what we'll do. You be at the Greyhound bus station in Oakland at ten A.M. tomorrow. I'll arrive there with a lovely brunet and we'll take the manuscript from its locker. It will be on the floor level, but there are hundreds of lockers there so you'll have to pay attention. I'll have the *Chronicle*'s sporting green sticking out of my left hip pocket."

"Left hip pocket," Piper repeated.

I found myself thinking, "Peter Piper picked a peck of pickled . . ." etc.

"Okay, now listen carefully," I said. I could hear his ice cubes again. Nick either must be able to hold his booze or he was getting a hell of a load on. "After the brunet and I leave, you keep an eye on the locker door. In a minute or less a man will check the locker. He'll be in a hurry because he'll be assigned to tail me. You wait until after he leaves the station, then you go to the locker. You with me?"

"Wait until he leaves."

"Okay, you go to the locker and on the top rear, held in place by a magnet, you'll find Shakespeare's one-page foul copy and the first page of the manuscript itself. You'll have five hours to find out if they're real or bogus. Leave yourself time to get to the train station and book an Amtrak liner north to Seattle. Can you do all that? Oh, yes, and bring along Xerox copies of your two sheets of paper."

"I can do it," said Piper. "Xeroxes too."

"The train leaves at three P.M. I'll meet you in the club car a half hour later. If I don't show at the lockers in the morning, I'll call you tomorrow night."

"See you tomorrow."

I hung up. I had taken a hell of a chance, but I didn't have any other choice. I had a feeling about him. He was okay.

My next stop was a department store where I bought a stuffed Winnie the Pooh, a manila envelope, and a package of typewriter paper. I palmed a kid's magnet on the side. I gave the Winnie back to the salesgirl.

"Listen," I said, "there will be a man in here in a few minutes wondering what I bought. I want you to give him this Pooh and tell him I bought it for his girl friend, if he has one."

The salesgirl giggled. "Are you serious?"

"Will you do that for me?" I gave her a couple of bucks.

"Sure," she said.

I left the store grinning like a fool.

Philip Boylan was parked in front of Katheryn and Helen's apartment when I drove up. He pretended not to notice me when I double-parked by the open window of his car. He started to turn the ignition key, but I motioned for him to stop.

"Listen," I said, "there's no need to hurry away. The fun will begin in the morning, and if you should get lost in the confusion, you might buy a ticket on the three P.M. Amtrak north."

Boylan looked amazed. That's the only way I can describe it.

"Why are you telling me this?" he asked.

"Because you're a real sport, Sheriff. You've come along this far, you might as well go the rest of the way."

I put my Fiat in gear and left him there to think about it. He'd be there.

CHAPTER 11

A sign by the apartment said there was Ample Parking. Since I drove a Fiat and not an Ample, I should have lodged a complaint against discrimination. The lot was full anyway, so I parked across the street.

I rang the doorbell and Helen answered. Katheryn looked up from the sofa where she sat squat-legged, reading a magazine with the face of a gorgeous girl on the front cover. The model looked right at the reader; a spot of light reflected off the cornea of each of her eyes. I once read somewhere that a magazine cover with reflected light on the model's eyeballs sold better than one without the spots.

Of course there were still Helen's eyes; they were still hazel and watched me with a look that was both relieved and cautious.

"We thought you'd never come back! What happened?" she asked. She brushed away a strand of dark hair that had strayed across her face—a lovely gesture, very female, and I watched with something approaching regret.

After my talk with the second Katheryn, I had to face a truth about myself.

Women such as Helen, even Yakima Helens, do not tumble eagerly into the arms of John Denson.

If she were interested, I could show her how to sketch rimrock in the high desert of eastern Oregon. I could show her how to carve a mallard drake out of a hunk of sugar pine. I could show her how to retrieve a bass plug on a hot August afternoon with beer waiting on shore in a styrofoam cooler. I could give her my lecture on the aesthetics of vegetable displays in farmer's markets—if she were interested.

It would take one hell of a willing suspension of disbelief to conclude that Helen would rather admire a stack of tomatoes than split a million and half bucks.

So she wouldn't care a whole lot about eating raw cauliflower or watching me fumble around with a thirty-five horsepower Evinrude? What the hell; I had my night and it had been lovely. I had one more night coming. What difference did it make if it was a charade by my partner? Maybe there was a hint of chemistry there after all. Just maybe. It was nice to think so anyway.

"I asked what happened, John."

I gave her my idea of a charming grin. John Denson, absentminded flake. "Sorry, I'm still having a time putting all the pieces together. Well, we drank a little draft Guinness in a fancy place where the waitresses wore no bras; we threw darts; we had a nice chat. I was apparently the only guy in the place who liked ladies' fronts. Sir Giles offered to match your price, but I said no."

Right then it was that I wished I was somewhere else. Walking down one of those Winslow Homer beaches maybe, with a surf rod in one hand, a bag of stale sandwiches in the other, and my eye on a distant rainsquall, the kind Homer suggested so nicely with a hint of Payne's gray. I wanted to tell the girls that—how I could never get the hang of bleeding a squall across the lighter gray of the sky so I fished instead and laid down the washes in my mind's eye.

"I was thinking how the British have a tradition of being good watercolorists. It's marvelous how they can give you a cow in a distant glade with a squiggle of color."

"You talked about watercolors?" asked Helen. Her eyes opened wide as she asked the question.

Katheryn's light dress was hiked up high on her thighs; I moved a fraction to my left. I had seen her dancing naked and here I was trying to get an angle on her underwear. It didn't make any sense. But if you believe Jim Bouton, a whole lot of men have the same habit.

Katheryn shifted her legs. I began my maneuvering all over again.

I gave up on getting an angle on Katheryn and perched atop the stool in the corner of the room that served as a kitchen. I tilted the stool until my back rested against the refrigerator. "We didn't talk about watercolors, but I imagine we could have. It would be part of Sir Giles's breeding to know about English artists. Mostly we talked about old times."

The girls didn't say anything. They just watched and waited for me to finish. They had offered their bodies as I had offered the steelhead those gaudy flies at Steamboat.

Now they were judging their fish, estimating his size and strength and whether he would run deep and hard in the depths of the drift or would come to the top, twisting, his silver body flashing in the sunlight.

The steelhead were smarter than I was.

But I was coming around.

"Sir Giles and I crossed paths once before. It was when I was in the intelligence business. I was sent to London to scratch an Englishman who had stolen some of our defense secrets. But I botched the job. I think I did it deliberately, but I wasn't ever sure. I'm still not to this very day. Anyway, a friend of mine made the hit. Twigg-Pritchart's men got even six months later."

"That's true?" asked Katheryn.

God, she had lovely legs. "It's the reason why I'm still not one of Sam's boys," I said. "I went to work for newspapers for a few years, dropped out of that too." I sensed that it was time now to make my move. I took care of an itch in my left armpit and continued. "Although I couldn't bring myself to murder a man in cold blood for something the British would discover themselves in another ten years, I was good at my work. My superiors tended to be educated in the better schools and found me amusing. I used to skip out to Chincoteague on the Virginia coast to fish for flounder and sea trout. I'll tell you right now, I know the players and the game. There's no sense putting it off; we may as well move the manuscript tomorrow."

By the players, I'm sure the girls assumed I meant Sir Giles and his men, Sheriff Boylan, and the FBI. It would never occur to girls who made their living dancing naked in front of helpless men that my intelligence could overcome the influence of my testicles.

They were almost right.

"What do you have in mind?" Katheryn asked.

"I don't imagine you would agree to the best way. That would be for you to give me the key to the locker at the bus terminal and the three of us go separate ways and rendezvous at three P.M. for the Amtrak liner heading north to Portland and Seattle.."

"You're right, we wouldn't agree," said Helen.

I ignored her. "As I said, that would be the smart way. Sir Giles has talked the FBI into leaving the manuscript to him. He told them it was a British national treasure and all that. Sir Giles does have men following me. If we split up, we weaken their ability to follow us."

"One of us has to be with you when you pick up the play," said Katheryn.

"Second best," I continued, "is for Helen and me to pick up the manuscript, do our best to lose our friends, and meet you at the Amtrak station for the three P.M. train north. That way we at least split their strength."

"Why the train?"

"Because if we do lose them, that's our best way out of town. Unless we're foolish enough to use a credit card, they won't have any way of knowing whether or not we're on board. That's not true of an airplane. If we don't lose them, we have an all-night train ride ahead of us with several stops along the way and a whole lot of options to consider."

"Do you think we'll lose them?"

"I wouldn't make book on it, but they won't get the manuscript."

"Then let's do it," Katheryn said.

I should have felt guilty about going to bed with Helen that night, but I didn't. Women like Helen wound up on the arms of neurosurgeons, rising young lawyers, and others who used their intelligence to make money rather than squandering it on odd notions of honor and justice. It was only fair that a John Denson should occasionally have his turn.

I slid into her arms as though I had been doing it for years, and the softness and warmth were as no other.

She fell asleep afterward, but I lay there and listened to the city sounds of San Francisco. The burden of a romantic is hard to bear.

But the city sounds soon receded into the distance and were replaced by the water of the North Umpqua sliding gently by me in the night. Helen's warm body was replaced by the dead girl who saved my life in the white water.

* * *

It was time for promises and pledges. Time to find out for certain who killed the girl on the river. Time to find out about William Shakespeare and Edward de Vere. Time to find out who was Katheryn Marsden and who was not. I had gone to bed overwhelmed by my good fortune at being in bed with Helen. I was overwhelmed with possibilities of Katheryns and clovers. Sir Giles was somewhere smiling at the thought of that.

Pascal had it easy. All he had to decide was whether or not it made sense to believe in God. The way he saw it, there is either a God or there isn't, and you are unable to tell which alternative is true. If you don't believe there is a God and there is, you lose everything since happiness and eternal life are the possible rewards. But if you do believe there is a God and there isn't, you haven't lost anything.

I had to decide between two girls with clovers, a more difficult problem, I'm sure even Pascal would agree. Katheryn the dancer was still my client. I owed her the benefit of the doubt. If she was genuine, then Katheryn II was a British agent. If Katheryn the dancer was a fake, Katheryn II could be real or she could still be an agent. Katheryn the dancer won on two of the three combinations. I decided to take Pascal's advice and play it safe—until it was proven otherwise, I would operate on the assumption that Katheryn II was the British agent.

If she was, I would know soon enough. My choice of a train would force Sir Giles to drop her cover. He would ask himself why I chose a train. Not knowing the route north and so not considering my foolish move, he would conclude Portland or Seattle. Trains stop downtown in both places. I knew Portland and Seattle well. My advantage. If Katheryn II joined Carder as an obvious tail on Katheryn, Helen, and me, Sir Giles could afford to keep secret the identity of his backup agents. He would have every agent ready to cover my moves. His advantage.

Besides, Katheryn II had served her purpose. She was, I was convinced, an imaginative gambit that appealed to Sir Giles's sense of humor. He might later describe her to his cronies at the club as a marvelous idea that just didn't work. "Imagine," he might tell his listeners, brushing a nonexistent speck from his impeccable vest, "just imagine the look on Denson's face, poor bastard, when he discovered that there was not just one, but two girls in the world with a birthmark in the shape of a four-leaf clover on the most intimate portion of her derriere." He might even affect a stutter, as members of the British upper class often do, and pronounce it "ba-ba-ba-bastard."

So even if it didn't work, the Katheryn II ploy would be worth it to Sir Giles. It would never occur to him that I might be ahead of him or even beat him; he would consider her pose harmless enough, an amusing episode in his adventure among the hayseeds and provincials. That it might unnecessarily demean her to no purpose was beside the point. What was a bun among friends? She was a professional.

I fell asleep and dreamed about the girl on the North Umpqua.

CHAPTER 12

The next morning we made our move.

Or rather I made my move.

I hadn't been completely honest with Katheryn and Helen. There was no way in heaven's name I could put Helen through all the paces necessary to ditch trained British professionals. By myself, I'd give them a good run. But dragging a hank of hair? No way. The girls would have balked at my real plan, which was to get everybody aboard the Amtrak liner north and dance the Siskiyou Two-Step at the Oregon border.

That wasn't going to be any fun at all.

But it had to be done.

Right now my problem was getting the manuscript onto the train. The British were waiting to snatch my package and run if I gave them half a chance. The trick was to give them no chance at all. A snatch would be their first objective, but that could wait. Their second objective wouldn't. Under no circumstances would I be allowed to get near a mailbox.

It would be foolish even to try. That's one reason why

Sir Giles had left me in the game. He hoped I would spare him the embarrassing spectacle of a public bloodletting.

I had caught glimpses of three or four of Sir Giles's troops, but they were good and I never could be sure. But I did know Carder. He was burned. Sir Giles would put him on my tail this fine summer day. He would have orders to stay there like a leech. The others were backups. I didn't mind. I respected Carder. He was a professional. It obviously rankled him to be assigned a mission whose sole purpose was to placate Sir Giles's ego.

The girls carried their cosmetics and mine plus a change of underwear in their handbags. I told Katheryn to go to the movies or shopping—have a good time—and not to pay any attention to people following her. All she had to do was show up at the Oakland rail terminal on time.

Katheryn didn't have a car, so I parked my Fiat in her apartment slot. We said our good-byes and Helen and I took a taxi to the bus station. The taxi driver, a young man with a full beard and long hair, gave Helen the eye in the rearview mirror. She ignored him and we sat in silence across the bay bridge. We had a tough day ahead of us. The trick was to pick up the manuscript at 10 A.M. and hold onto it until the 3 P.M. departure of the Amtrak liner north.

Katheryn said the manuscript was genuine, and I didn't have any reason not to believe her until the appearance of Katheryn II. Besides, Sam taught me never to leave anything to chance. Never. Ever. The five hours would give Nick Piper time to check the authenticity of the foul paper and the first page of the manuscript.

I had the beard stop the taxi two blocks short of the bus station. I bought a *Chronicle* and an *Enquirer* from a newsstand and strolled leisurely the rest of the way, flipping through my papers. The *Enquirer* had a picture of Elliott Gould and a new girl friend on the cover. My encounter on the North Umpqua was detailed on the inside, illustrated with an artist's conception of Denson atop a nude girl. It looked like I was either groping her awkwardly or copulating, take your pick. Fornicating in white water is not a trick included in *The Joy of Sex*. The *Chronicle* had a good story too. Seems a nearsighted fly fisherman on the North Umpqua had stumbled onto the bloated bodies of Anston and Edith Marsden.

Oh, boy. I kept the *Enquirer* for future laughs and threw everything in the *Chronicle* away except the sporting green. I folded the green and stuck it in my left hip pocket for Nick Piper's benefit.

The bus station was an old building with marble floors, old-fashioned benches, and high ceilings that picked up every sound and caused it to echo, echo, echo. The air was heavy with the odor of pine oil, wine, and human sweat. It was a rest stop for people from nowhere going nowhere. An adolescent male with trousers too short for his long legs listened to rock music on a transistor radio. A girl with braces on her teeth and breasts so large they embarrassed her sat with a plastic purse and a shoe box and stared at nothing. A wino in a Goodwill costume watched a spot on the floor. A grandmother from down in Fresno, up to see her daughter and grandson, fidgeted with a needlepoint project. Her daughter was late and the old lady was frightened. Another wino squatted in a corner with a bottle in a paper bag.

This, then, was where William Shakespeare's lost comedy was stashed.

I scanned the winos, waiters, and dreamers, trying to spot my man Nick Piper. It was impossible to tell which one of the older men was he.

The pale green lockers were the only thing new about the station. They had apparently replaced an older generation of lockers that had seen their day. I strode across the marble floor with Helen on my arm. She led me straight to the appropriate bank of lockers. She carried her handbag. I had a leather briefcase that locked, with a dummy envelope, a pair of handcuffs, and my magnet inside.

We walked casually down a wall of lockers until Helen paused and said, "This one." She nudged a floor locker with her foot and gave me the key.

I turned and gave a Boy Scout salute to Carder, who sat on a bench not twenty feet away.

Carder acknowledged with a nod.

I retrieved my handcuffs from the leather briefcase, slipping one end over my wrist and securing the other to the handle of the briefcase. I squatted, slipped Helen's key into the locker, and opened it.

The manuscript was in a large manila envelope that was similar enough to the dummy in my briefcase.

I turned my back on Carder and slipped the envelope quickly into my open briefcase. Then, still squatting, I pivoted on my heels so Carder could see. I withdrew both envolopes from the briefcase and gave one to Helen.

"Take this please and walk very quickly, I say very quickly, toward the express package window. Our friend will stop you halfway there, but that's okay. Give him the envelope. Go." I gave her a whack on the rump. She went.

Carder looked startled at the sight of two envelopes.

I smirked.

"You're better off staying right where you are, lad," he warned and went after Helen.

I stayed. I opened the envelope with the manuscript, withdrew and folded once the top two papers, and stuck them to the top rear of the locker with the magnet. Everything went right. I didn't fumble. The magnet did its job.

Helen and Carder were on their way back by the time I had turned around. Carder had the dummy envelope in his hand.

I gave them a great big smile. "It's all here," I said.

Carder ignored that. "What was that little diversion all about?" he asked. He looked puzzled.

"I needed a few seconds to see if I had the real goods."

Carder still looked puzzled. He was a professional; he had to be satisfied with an answer. He wasn't satisfied with mine.

"Your problem is that you think too much, Mr. Carder."

He smiled. "Is that possible, Mr. Denson?" He returned to his place on the bench.

I slid the hand with the handcuff key into my left pocket and bent to tie my shoelace. I dropped the key into my shoe.

The loudspeaker announced the pending arrival of a bus from Sacramento and points north. When the announcement was finished, I smiled at Carder. "I don't think you'll be able to pull a snatch in a public place, Mr. Carder. Sir Giles authorize hardware if I should try for a mailbox?"

Carder nodded his head yes.

"Have a nice day," I said. I tripped against the edge of the bench as I turned, sending the key to the toe of my shoe.

"There's no way the two of us can lose Carder," I told Helen. "He has two or three agents backing him. They'll be watching the entrances and exits right now. If I try to get smart, I'm liable to lose my wrist in addition to the briefcase."

Helen swallowed. "What do we do?" she asked. She looked over her shoulder at Carder.

"We move and move quickly," I said.

Carder flipped open the door of the locker, gave a quick glance to make sure it was empty, and hurried to catch up. Now he was strolling placidly along looking every bit the junior executive. Some lucky mom's boy who was doing okay by himself.

"What we do is find some nice public place and wait it

out until train time. Train time is when John Denson does his magic act."

Helen raised her eyebrow. "Oh, yeah?"

"That's it," I said. "Fake the bloody Brits right out of their wing tips."

Across the street an entire block had been razed to make way for a parking lot as part of an urban renewal project. At least that's what the sign said. All that was left of what once must have been a fine old hotel were a few scattered bricks, most of them broken. A group calling itself the People's Coalition for a Better Oakland was camped on the lot, offering a People's Renaissance Fair. It featured food stalls of one sort or another, various arts and crafts such as bad oil paintings, a few fair watercolors, pottery that all looked the same, brass belt buckles with the same designs, some handweaving with crooked warps, and a young man playing a dulcimer, accompanied by a comely lady playing a washtub bass.

"There," I said. "We wait there."

"That looks like lots of fun," said Helen.

"There's no accounting for taste, I guess."

I picked an improvised outdoor Mexican café that was strong on refried beans and Spanish rice but weak on enchiladas, tacos, and almost everything else. It did serve beer and it had faded canvas parasols over the tables for shade. I was not attracted by the beans. What caught my eye was a stall next door in which an enterprising young photographer was willing—for the nothing price of $4.50—to take your picture in a wild West costume. The result was a browned, stilted photograph intended to resemble Mathew Brady's Civil War efforts.

His business was not brisk.

He raised his eyebrows and pulled at his scraggly red beard when I offered him twenty bucks to photograph anybody who approached me other than the waiters he recognized.

"The twenty is just for keeping your eyes open. I'll give you another ten for each shot you actually take."

His eyes narrowed. "You ain't fuzz, are you?"

"The very opposite."

"Cool."

I slipped him the twenty and waved at Carder, who waited at a respectful distance.

"What did you do that for?" Helen asked when we sat down.

"So we can have some privacy while we wait, my love."

She had amber flecks in her hazel eyes.

"Oh, you're just a smooth talker, you are," she said. "How long do we wait?"

I ordered a pitcher of beer and two glasses. "We wait until it's time to go the train station. We drink beer. I watch unwashed girls with no bras and unshaved armpits. You worry about the bad guys. Come lunchtime we'll eat what we can of a pool of refried beans on a paper plate and maybe have a bad enchilada or two. After lunch we'll drink more beer. I'll watch more unwashed girls with no bras and unshaved armpits. You'll continue to fret about the bad guys."

"I can't wait."

"On the other hand—" I said. I gave her a fine leer. "We can sit here adjusting our chairs to keep out of the sun and be romantic lovers as the dulcimer and washtub bass play our songs."

"Oh, boy," she said and shifted her chair.

The dulcimer and washtub bass didn't stay forever. They were soon replaced by fiddlers. Street people then appeared from everywhere and began to leap and bound around in the hot sun in what they apparently believed was the manner of a western hoedown. The males of the species concentrated on raising their sandaled feet as high off the pavement as they could. They moved around their ladies in great, frenzied, high-kicking circles with their chests out, chins high, and long hair flowing. The women spun their skirts enthusiastically so that onlookers were treated to a full view of pantied behinds. The behinds tended to be either emaciated from a diet of brown rice and yogurt or plump from eating cheap starches. There seemed few in between. The fiddlers retired and were replaced by black men with drums. The blacks wore colorful dashikis and pounded on their drums like men possessed. When they finished, the white members of the audience were ostentatiously energetic in their applause. Palms were swollen from the accolade. The drummers weren't bad, actually. But they weren't that good.

Helen was an enthusiastic spectator. She admired everything except the small children who were allowed to wander naked, dirty, and unattended through the crowd.

"It's the natural way. Organic," I said when she asked where the mothers were. Here was a woman who danced naked one day and fretted about small children the next.

By one o'clock there wasn't a whole lot of shade left under the parasol, but we endured. We were treated, in turn, to a tone-deaf yodeler, a belly dancer with a stomach that rolled like the surf off Makapuu, jugglers, a harmonica band, flutists, a thin girl with a Jew's harp, an evangelist of some sort who warned us that fornication would send us to perdition, a representative of the Bay Area Gay Liberation Front, and a girl promoting the marvelous qualities of a douche scented with rose hips.

Although it was party line for the People's Coalition for a Better Oakland to despise free enterprise in all its vile forms, nobody objected to a little hustling so long as General Motors was not involved. But so what? What did it matter? I don't like General Motors either. And everybody was having such a good time.

What bothered me, I guess, was the sight of so many young people squandering their youths on delusions.

At about two o'clock, though, I began to get nervous. It wasn't from fatigue, dehydration, or the refried beans. It was because of the apparently long-awaited rock group called Judah's Truth. The Truth brought with them an incredible sound system. It was called, I suspect accurately enough, "Echos of the Cosmos." The speakers—bizarre testaments to man's ingenuity—were six to eight feet wide. And there were twelve of them.

I began to fear for that part of my anatomy called the tympanic membrane, which the folks call the eardrum.

"My God, you don't suppose they're actually going to plug that thing in, do you?" asked Helen.

"I'm not sure it would work. I think they'd have to have a direct link to Hoover Dam," I said.

"Would you look at that! The musicians are ignored. The technicians have the groupies with the nubile bodies."

"Those are called nubies in the business," I said.

"What?"

"Never mind."

The much-admired technicians struggled with enormous electrical wires that looked like trans-Atlantic cables. Any manner of developing fourteen-year-olds scrambled about eager to be of help.

I looked at my watch. It was 2:30 P.M. Time to go.

Carder appeared from nowhere as we moved off to catch a taxi. He looked relieved.

And for a moment concerned. Tailing automobiles in traffic is a risky business. But everything went well for the Englishman. Carder's backup moved up quickly and picked him up in a Datsun. The Datsun swung smartly in behind our taxi, a Plymouth with a hundred sixty thousand miles on the speedometer.

The train station was more elaborate than the bus depot, but was not what you would call elegant. It lacked the depot's winos, and that was a saving grace. A pretty girl at the ticket window was trying to emulate those sleek but distant women who work at airline terminals. I wanted to tell her I liked her a whole lot better, even though she had gone to a community college and hadn't been taught the correct way to walk. I like unrestricted, uneducated behinds that roll and twitch this way and that.

She was eager to help us and smiled a real smile.

I reserved a sleeper space and coach seats for three. We lined up to get on the train.

It was not a large train. There was an Amtrak diesel up front, followed by four coach cars, one club car, one dining car, and two sleepers.

Katheryn II, carrying the latest issue of *Cosmopolitan*, followed us on board. I turned and leered suggestively at her, but she stared right through me with a blank look.

I wasn't sure, but I thought I saw the corner of her mouth move just a trifle. I knew if I really tried I could make her laugh, but I didn't want to embarrass her in front of her fellow agents. They had no doubt already given her the raspberry about her fake birthmark.

I wanted to lean over and whisper, "I know a secret about you."

When we got on the coach, I chose seats in the rear of the third coach to make things tough on her. She would have preferred to sit behind us, but was forced to sit in front. She would have also preferred some room between us and the club car.

CHAPTER 13

It would be a long night on the Amtrak run. We would roll north past vineyards, truck farms, and tangles of freeways where tourists would be laboring under the late-afternoon sun, competing with big rigs loaded with California vegetables. We would pass the Sacramento River and the American River. We would see Lassen and Shasta bathed in crimson with the setting sun. The Sierra Nevadas behind them would blue to infinity as they stretched north to become the Cascade Range. Then we would slow for the ascent of the Siskiyous before we pushed on through primeval forests of Douglas fir. It would be night then and the ridges of trees would be shadows in the blackness.

There, somewhere, truth would come.

We waited in our seats and relaxed until, with an unexpected suddenness, the train began to glide north out of the confusion of rails that was the Oakland terminal. The interior of the coach was Amtrak's best effort to emulate the sterile comfort of an airliner. The decorator had chosen Muzak tones of soft maroons and muted grays. The yards outside were blackened by the exhaust of generations of diesel engines. There was no color. None. A splash of burnt umber would have dazzled the eye.

The train accelerated swiftly once we left Oakland and began to rock gently from side to side as we moved across the Berkeley Mud Flats and past the oil refineries. The bay was to our left and across it, San Francisco. The campus of the University of California was on the hills to our right.

When we were out of the bay, I unlocked my briefcase and got out *Jonathan Claiborne*.

"What are you going to do?" Katheryn looked alarmed.

"I'm going to read Shakespeare's play. Don't worry, nobody's going to take it away from me sitting in a car full of people." The manuscript was fragile but in surprisingly good shape. I'd have to be careful.

"Maybe you better sit on the window side."

"If it makes you feel better." We switched seats.

I'm not an English professor, but I thought *Claiborne* made good reading. Shakespeare in effect compared the hangers-on of a Carolina chief named Matuseh with the Elizabethan court. The English came off second best. There was also a love affair between James Barrett, Claiborne's lecherous but proper secretary, and Matuseh's handsome daughter, Tipaweena. The chief was opposed to the match because the British were uncivilized. Matuseh said all those European clothes would make Tipaweena sweat too much: She would bear stunted children and die an early death. Barrett fashioned her a blouse to shield her breasts from his fellow travelers.

Shakespeare had a way of suddenly being serious in the middle of a comedy. Maybe comedy is serious business, I don't know. In a discussion of primitive customs, Claiborne observed that all men dance from the moment of birth. "The Lady watches whilst we prance." The line stayed with me as I sat there on that gently rocking train. Old Bill knew his stuff.

I put the manuscript back in the briefcase and locked it. "I'm going to the club car to have a drink and think things through. You two watch the briefcase. Leave it locked. Stay together and nothing will happen to it. Okay?"

"Okay," Helen said.

When I left them they were watching the scenery slide past. Two lovely girls on a train ride. A tranquil scene.

I shouldered my way past the door to the club car, which was hard to open, and when I stepped inside I saw him immediately.

Professor Nicholas Piper.

He was five feet seven or eight inches tall, overweight for his size. He was in his mid-sixties. He wore sturdy shoes chosen for comfort rather than style. It was hard to understand his taste in clothes. Since he was a full professor, I didn't imagine he was completely broke. Yet his jacket was at least fifteen years out of date and had seen hard use in its day. His tie, a manure color, was decorated with a yellow stain and lay askew on his stomach, revealing an unfastened shirt button.

Piper had gray hair that was long about the ears. He had a round face with a nose that turned up slightly at the end. He either had a fast-growing beard or a dull razor. He squinted at me in recognition through small eyes under bushy eyebrows that other men would have trimmed.

"Ah, John, good to see you, good to see you." Piper rose slightly, steadying himself with his left hand.

"I'm glad to see everything went well," I said. "You were the wino squatting with the bag, right?"

Piper laughed. "How did I look?"

"You looked just fine or else you wouldn't be here looking so cheery."

"Lovely ride. Last time I was through this country was in 1937. I was working on a layout for *Life* magazine." He took a sip of martini and the tinkle of ice was familiar from the night before. "Would you like a drink?"

"Why not?"

Piper signaled for a waiter, and a few minutes later I was sipping Coors beer.

"What did you find, Nick?"

"I'm not sure, but I think I found out you were ahead of both me and our friend Twigg-Pritchart as well. I took the foul copy and the first page of the play to Levi Goldman at Berkeley. What we have, John, is a convincing bogus manuscript. It took Levi hours with his chemicals to find that out." Piper marked the period with a sip of his martini.

I couldn't help laughing. "Well, you said yourself Sayani was a clever student."

Piper chuckled. "Not *that* damned clever, for Christ's sake."

"Sir Giles and his friends are in one of the coaches up front. So is my pal, Sheriff Boylan . . ."

"The one who checked into Sayani's room after Mohan's unfortunate encounter with the prostitute."

"The very same," I said. I ordered another Coors. "What I propose, Nick, is that we get justice for the dead girl on the North Umpqua."

Piper leaned over the table and took a sip of martini. "As per your statements to the paper."

"Exactly. It's not that I feel Zane Grey's drift will be permanently sullied by the unrevenged death of the girl, but the very real fact that her corpse saved my life."

"I see," said Piper. He nodded solemnly.

"Plus, enough jack to buy me a fishing boat, you a whole bunch of books if that's your druthers, and the two girls back there a vacation in France or someplace where wealthy young men with sports cars hang out."

Piper brightened. "How would you do that?"

"First off, did you Xerox your stuff as I asked?"

"Done. Brought originals and copies with me."

"Good. Now, what if the foul copy and the first page were genuine but all that remained of the play was a Xerox copy?"

Piper brightened even more. "Then the foul copy, that one page plus the photocopied play, would bring almost as much as the complete original on the market."

It looked like Piper had drooled egg yolk on his tie, but I couldn't be sure. "How long did it take your Berkeley friend to find out it was bogus?"

"The better part of three hours, and that's with an expensive laboratory at his disposal."

"I assume you get my drift."

"How could I not get your drift? What do you say we drink to it?" Piper grinned broadly.

"Certainly," I said. We toasted, plastic glass of beer to plastic glass of martini.

"And what would you think would be our next step?"

"To arrange for our friend Sir Giles to steal the play from poor Katheryn, who's sitting back there with visions of designer originals, trinkets by De Beers, and a gorgeous home overlooking the Big Sur. I can't tell the girls because we'll need their tortured weeping and wailing to pull it off."

"Ouch," said Piper. His face registered pain.

"The screaming may be a trifle much, but we'll have to endure. In the end it's the only way they'll even see part of their treasure."

"What do I do now?"

"You wait, Nick. I'm going back to see how they're doing. I'll propose that Katheryn go to the ladies' john and check the manuscript to make sure it's all there."

"What will happen then?" Piper took a healthy slug of martini.

"I'm not certain, but I'll just bet a brunet girl in the employ of Her Majesty's Government will casually follow her inside and take it away. She may put poor Katheryn to sleep for a few minutes, but she'll recover. By that time Twigg-Pritchart will be reading *Jonathan Claiborne* and wondering why I let Katheryn pull such a stunt."

"What'll you say to that?"

"Why, I'll blame it on a dumb broad, what else?"

Piper grinned. "He'll also be wondering what happened to the first page."

"Professor Piper, I think you're in the wrong business," I said.

"There's only one thing that puzzles me."

"What's that?"

Piper cleared his throat. "Tell me what you would have done if the manuscript had been genuine?"

I grinned. "I'd have danced my little dance."

Piper laughed. "What the hell's that?"

"That, professor, is the one thing I keep to myself until the time comes. It's not that I don't trust you; I do. But my little dance is one thing I can't risk being telegraphed. I can never tell what's gonna happen."

Piper thought that over. "You're the professional; I'll follow your advice. But would you tell me about the brunet whom you're so sure will lift the play for Twigg-Pritchart? How did you know about her? Did she follow you today?"

I finished the last of my second beer. "That's a long story, Nick. Just say she's a hell of an actress with a sweet tush. I'd better go back there and get things moving."

I returned to the coach where Katheryn and Helen were reading magazines. Katheryn said it made sense to check the manuscript. She went forward to the ladies' toilet. I went to the rear and the club car and Nick Piper's company.

Neither Nick nor I said anything. We just sat and waited as the gently rocking Amtrak liner carried us by grazing cattle, fields of alfalfa, and handsome barns. An elderly couple in an old pickup waited patiently at one crossing.

Interstate highways are bordered by truck stops, billboards, curio shops, and fast-food restaurants. Trains are different. A train is an irregular visitor to the fields and stretches of wilderness. The people and cattle, sheep, dogs, and deer have learned to ignore them. Farm boys are lulled to sleep by the gentle rocking and clacking of distant trains.

No farm boy would be lulled to sleep by the vision of Helen as she stepped into the club car.

"It's gone, John," she said. Tears started coming and she wiped them away with the back of her arm.

"What's gone?"

"The play. Katheryn went to the toilet to check the manuscript. A woman sitting in front of us followed her into the toilet and pulled out a pistol. She took the manuscript, forced Katheryn to take off her clothes, then stepped out of the door and was gone. By the time Katheryn got dressed, the woman had disappeared to the front of the train." Helen began to cry and in the middle of her crying was overtaken by a series of great hiccups that shook her torso. "It is, *hic*, gone, *hic*. More than a million, *hic*, dollars!"

If I had just lost that much money I would have hiccuped too. Yet I couldn't help but admire Katheryn II. She knew her women. Katheryn danced naked for a living, but would lose a million and a half bucks rather than step nude into the corridor of an Amtrak coach and yell for help.

Sir Giles now had the manuscript. The next move was mine. John Denson, cool private investigator. Yes, sir. On top of everything.

"Listen," I said. "This man's name is Nicholas Piper. You stay with him while I talk to Katheryn. This may be just a minor setback, you never know."

"Bullshit, it's gone," she said. No hics interrupted that statement.

"Where's Katheryn now?"

"She's still, *hic*, in the toilet, *hic*. Crying her guts out."

When I stepped into the coach, there was no mistaking the fact that Katheryn or Margo, or whoever, was still in the toilet. All eyes in the coach were turned in the direction of the tortured wails coming from inside the women's toilet. An Amtrak conductor was standing in the narrow passageway pounding on the door.

"Is there any way I can be of assistance, ma'am?" he yelled at the door.

He was answered by renewed wailing. The girl had lungs.

"Please, ma'am," he pleaded.

I took a turn. I rapped softly on the door and said, "It's me, John Denson. Everything is not lost, do you hear me? Everything is not lost."

The door opened and Katheryn stared at me through reddened eyes. "Just what in the hell do you mean, 'everything is not lost?' That bitch shoved a pistol in my face, forced me to strip, and walked off with *Jonathan Claiborne*!"

The conductor, sensing the racket had been quelled, moved judiciously off down the coach. I said to Katheryn, very softly so that no one else could conceivably hear, "That play was a fake, Margo; it wasn't worth two cents. If we play our cards right, we can still wangle a bundle for both you and Helen. You can help out by continuing to wail. Don't stop for twenty minutes or until your throat gives out, whichever comes first."

She grinned. "Boy, you're a real son of a bitch, do you know that? I think we had you underestimated all down the line. You knew all along that I wasn't Katheryn Marsden, didn't you?"

"No, not until I learned the play was fake. But I still think that fake birthmark was awfully cute. So it's Margo Kiner, isn't it? Your real name?"

"It's Margo," she said.

"Well, what the hell! That isn't such a bad name."

"Are you ready for the wailing?"

"Let 'er rip," I said. I knew she could do it, judging from her performance that first morning in her apartment.

Margo wailed. Not a little bit, but honest to God, gut-wrenching, wracking, anguished sobs. Great stuff. I shrugged my shoulders and headed back toward the club car. I met the conductor halfway there. He looked crestfallen that the wailing had resumed.

"Jesus Christ, I'll never understand women," I said.

The conductor gave me a sympathetic look. "She sounds like a real dandy."

I didn't know about that. But she sure as hell could scream.

CHAPTER 14

Margo made a good run at my suggested twenty minutes, but exhaustion set in before she could meet her goal. I'm sure everybody on the train figured her to make the *Guinness Book of World Records.*

Afterward she joined Nick, Helen, and me in the club car, where we all had a drink and I explained our situation.

"It was a fake, all the time a fake," said a disconsolate Helen.

Margo was enraged that I had set her up in the john.

"You set me up, you bastard! You knew I'd get ripped off if I went in there alone. Say, how was it you knew she was working for Sir Giles anyway?"

"Yeah, that's a question," said Helen.

If Nick and I had convinced them that the play was bogus, they weren't so sure now.

I told them about Katheryn II, she of the sweet British tush.

Helen raised her left eyebrow. "Exactly how good was she, John?"

I caught a hint of jealousy there. Made me feel good as hell. "No treats, just a peek, that's all. A nice little behind it was, complete with a fake birthmark, just like Margo's here. Can you people tell me where the real Katheryn Marsden is?"

"She's in Tokyo at a meeting of the PEN. She's not due back until next week," said Helen. "We had her apartment rented for the summer."

"And Oriana Kauffmann. Is there such a person?"

"Certainly, but she isn't your dead girl. She's visiting her parents in New Jersey for a month. One of Bill's best Bawdies. Packs 'em in. We made up all that stuff about her disappearing for two days. Once we were threatened and knew what the package was worth, we wanted to get into the action."

Nick Piper grinned and shook his head. He had himself a tad more martini.

I started to continue, but Helen motioned for me to stop. "Oh, no, you don't. It's your turn to answer some questions, fast John."

"You Yakima girls are tough. By the way, where are you from, Margo?"

"Fresno, and don't laugh."

"You see me laughing? I'm from a place called Cayuse on the banks of the Columbia River."

"I have an English degree from San Jose State. They have professors there with Ph.D.'s and everything. And I agree with Helen."

"What's that?"

"It's your turn to answer some questions. Like when did you know Boylan brought the manuscript back from Honolulu?"

"When I read in a newspaper clip that he'd been questioned."

"When did you know Margo wasn't Katheryn Marsden?" asked Helen.

I grinned. "Well, as I told her back at the women's john, I really didn't until Nick told me the play was a fake. But having Margo pass her ass in review on that dancer's ramp was ingenious, I'll give you that. After all, what are the odds that there would be two women in the world with a birthmark like that on her bun? Then there was the business of Margo's offering to go to bed with me after I'd been with you. The two of you knew I wouldn't sleep with her. The newspapers told you what kind of person I was. I took Margo's offer as San Francisco chic, proof that she really was Katheryn. Would an impostor risk having her ass examined close up? No."

"What about the manuscript?" Margo asked. "When did you know that was a fake?"

"Just when I told you, not until I met Nick on the train. I had him check the play out as a matter of course. It had to be done. I began to wonder about it when I found out Sayani's professor was a professor."

Nick cleared his throat. "Then of course there's the question of what we do next."

I took a sip of beer. "Questions, Nick. There's the matter of conning Sir Giles with a bogus manuscript and there's the matter of the dead girl."

Margo shifted at the mention of the dead girl. It was okay for me to be gallant and all that, as long as it didn't cost her money. She was afraid it might. An understandable fear.

"Justice comes first, then money. Are we agreed?" I asked.

Piper answered without hesitation. "Absolutely."

"Yes," said Helen.

Margo wasn't so sure. "I don't know," she said.

I didn't want to argue. "Good, we're agreed. I'm going

to invite Sir Giles back here for a nice chat. The trick is to get the most we can with the cards we hold. That'll take a little bluffing. You girls are welcome to sit in while I do the talking. I may be a bit flaky, but I've been around men like Sir Giles: I know how they think. No matter what I say that might not square with the facts as you know them, be quiet. That's essential. Agreed?"

"Certainly," said Piper.

Helen nodded her head yes.

Margo didn't say anything.

"My guess is either Sir Giles or Boylan murdered the girl on the river. Since I don't know who she was, motives are hard to come by. If it was Sir Giles, we have a long night ahead. If it was Boylan, I'll make book Sir Giles knows what happened. The details will be part of our bargain for the manuscript. I'm going to shoot for a hundred and fifty grand for the four of us to split. Open your mouth at the wrong time and you can kiss it good-bye."

"We don't have any other choice, do we?" asked Margo.

"No," I said. "Nick, if I could please have a Xerox of our foul paper and the first page of Mr. Sayani's fine play? Thank you." I got a closer look at Nick's tie. It was egg yolk.

I had the feeling that Nick's getup was no disguise. This was genuine Piper.

Sir Giles Twigg-Pritchart was sitting with Carder two cars forward. He was reading *Jonathan Claiborne* when I paused in the aisle at his side, steadying myself with one hand against the rocking of the train.

"My gal couldn't overcome the temptation of sneeking a peek. Enjoy the play, Sir Giles?"

Sir Giles closed the manuscript on his lap and smiled. "The play appears genuine enough, but it's bad Shakespeare. That's probably the reason we don't find it in college textbooks today. Lost for a good reason, I'd say."

"Maybe it would be better with the first page." I squatted in the aisle for better balance.

Sir Giles did not appear concerned. "So you still have the first page, do you? I would judge that to be next to worthless on the market."

"We have the original first page and we have a Xerox of the rest of the play. Plus, we have the original of this." I handed him the Xerox of the foul paper. "That, as you can see, is a detailed note from the author to his scribe outlining changes to be made before the play was submitted to the Master of Revels."

Twigg-Pritchart looked mildly interested. "I see. But I'm not sure that I really care. What does it have to do with me? I see by the papers that Professor Marsden is dead."

"What it has to do with you is that it proves Marsden's point. Our foul paper and the first page of the play are enough to prove the authenticity of the complete Xeroxed manuscript. All that remains is a computer analysis."

Sir Giles grinned. "You don't seem to understand, Mr. Denson, that my quarrel was with Anston Marsden. I have the original. Let his philistine colleagues speculate if they choose."

I shifted my squat to a more comfortable position. "What you don't seem to understand, Sir Giles, is that the by-line above the definitive article on Shakespeare's identity won't be by one of Marsden's colleagues; it will be by Anston Marsden himself."

Sir Giles was, of course, enraged at my coup. He wasn't about to give Marsden's colleagues a chance to speculate. His scorn was bluff. But my last card was too much. His left eyebrow lifted slightly.

"How will that be done, may I ask?"

Carder looked properly concerned, but I caught his eye and saw a hint of amusement there. Carder wasn't all bad.

"Marsden's analysis is already programmed. An undergraduate can feed it into the machine. It's only proper that his byline go up top."

Sir Giles said nothing.

The train went *click, cl-click, cl-click.*

"If you would care to discuss the matter, we would like you to join us in the club car. We have a nice table there, plenty of room to accommodate yourself and Mr. Carder, or even the girl with the fake birthmark."

"Her name is Phoebe," said Carder. I caught a suggestion of proprietary interest.

"Actress, bandit, and possessor of a gorgeous behind," I said.

"I wouldn't know the details of the latter."

"I don't know a lot about it myself," I admitted. I wanted Carder on my side.

Sir Giles straightened and brushed at his trousers. "I shall be delighted to join your party," he said.

I led the way back, followed by Carder, Sir Giles, and eventually by Phoebe, who grinned and winked at me as she waited to join our procession. "How many more are you?" I asked over my shoulder.

"Three, assigned to various parts of the train, but they won't be joining us in the discussions," said Carder.

We settled around the largest table in the club car and introductions were made. Phoebe's last name, it turned out, was Smythe. Smythe, mind you, not Smith, which I had always thought was an honorable English name.

Twigg-Pritchart took a special interest in Nick Piper. "Ahh, Professor Piper, I'm pleased to meet you. My people tell me you have been imbibing with Mr. Denson. Have you two been acquainted long?"

Nick was momentarily flustered. He didn't know how much he should tell Sir Giles. He looked my way. I grinned and shrugged. It was a detail we had overlooked. Nick cleared his throat. "I contacted John through his answering service in Seattle. I was after the manuscript for Mohan Sayani, who is its owner. I called John yesterday and he said he already had clients but might need my help on the train today. He said he would be able to arrange a fee that would help with Sayani's education."

It was a perfect answer. Gorgeous. I breathed easier.

Sir Giles turned to me. It was my show. I was expected to lead the negotiations. I wasn't sure I was up to it. I was getting a bit high from the booze. When I get drunk, I become exuberant, expansive, and am given to bad jokes and coarse laughter.

This, obviously, was neither the time nor the place to lose my head.

I poured myself another plastic cup of Coors. "Friends, I propose that we toast the Union Jack and Old Glory." I held the plastic cup aloft and we had our toast. Of all the people around the table, Nick Piper was having the best time. He had a great, fine, happy grin on his face; he was having an adventure and wasn't going to let anything spoil it. Margo and Helen were quiet, worrying, I knew, that I might blow their last chance at a bundle. Phoebe sipped port and looked proper, as though she were discussing the Common Market at tea. Carder drank Scotch and said nothing. If he let his true feelings show, Sir Giles could screw him out of a promotion.

Sir Giles was still in the process of recovering from his latest setback. He ordered beer as well. He took a sip and watched me carefully.

Nobody said anything for several minutes. It was a lovely night outside. There was a pale moon. We could see the profiles of evergreens and the lights of an occasional isolated farmhouse. Nothing else. The Siskiyous would be coming in an hour or two. If push came to shove, I was ready to bolt the train on the slowdown in order to keep our bluff going. But I hoped it wouldn't come to that.

"Well now," I said. I paused, trying to remember if I had forgotten anything. I didn't think so. "We're here to negotiate the sale of a foul copy of instructions to a scribe in the hand of one Edward de Vere, also known as William Shakespeare."

Sir Giles gave me a bland look that betrayed no emotion whatever.

But I knew I had him.

"We're also here to balance the scales of justice in the death of a young woman I found floating in the river four days ago," I said. I looked at Sir Giles.

He said nothing. The train hit a bad stretch of track and the car lurched slightly.

"Well?" I asked.

"I'm not sure you'll want to know the details," he said mildly.

"That's all I've been after since I pulled her body out of the North Umpqua. I want them, all right, and you're not going to get what you want until I hear them."

"The lady's name was Susan Marsden," said Sir Giles. "She had a quarrel with her young man in Amsterdam. She returned to the United States and joined her parents in Eugene until Sheriff Boylan caught up with them."

I'd suspected as much. "Is Boylan on the train now?"

"In the lead coach, I suspect, waiting for you to get off the train with *Jonathan Claiborne.* I've a man watching him."

"Boylan, then the girl. What happened?"

Sir Giles, it was clear, wasn't eager to part with the details. "The Honolulu police suspected Boylan of walking off with the Goan's play from the start. He said he didn't have it. They didn't believe him. But what choice did they have?"

"Not much," I said.

Sir Giles grinned. "Precisely. There was, however, much *we* could attempt. My agents booked lodgings in a motel, put a tap on his phone, and went fishing. They tell me trout fishing on the North Umpqua is better than in Scotland. Well, they waited for some time, several weeks in fact, before Boylan contacted Marsden."

"You knew for certain Boylan had the manuscript?"

"Oh, yes, he negotiated Marsden's fee over the telephone."

"So Boylan took *Jonathan* to Eugene?"

Sir Giles nodded.

"Why didn't you take it away from him?"

He looked at Carder, who cleared his throat. "We were going to, but it was raining heavily and before we could find an opportune stretch on the freeway, Mr. Carder here managed to slide our vehicle off the road."

I had to laugh at that. So did Nick Piper. Even Carder managed a small grin. Sir Giles didn't think it especially funny.

"Well, we caught up with him in Eugene and the next morning Professor Marsden slipped the manuscript into a blue mailbox while I watched helplessly from across the street. Sheriff Boylan was enraged."

"I'll bet."

"He piled the three of them—Marsden, his wife, Edith, and his daughter Susan—into the back of his squad car and drove south."

"With you right behind," I said.

"That's right. It wasn't raining on the return trip and Mr. Carder here was able to keep our rented vehicle on the road. Boylan drove to the headwaters of the North Umpqua, to an area reserved for fly fishermen only."

That would be the area upstream from Steamboat. "What happened then?" I asked.

"I'm not certain you'll approve of this portion of my narrative."

"Keep talking."

Sir Giles smiled. "Well, Sheriff Boylan bound and gagged the parents. Then he stripped the girl." He stopped.

"And?"

"You have to understand we figured the stripping was for show." He stopped again.

"And what?"

Sir Giles took a deep breath. "The sheriff raped her."

"You didn't do anything?" Helen leaned across the table. She was wide-eyed with disbelief.

Sir Giles turned up the palms of his hands. "What could I do? She was only raped, after all. The man had a pistol. A rape is hardly sufficient reason for a gallant rescue with the possible loss of human life."

I started to interrupt, but an annoyed Sir Giles silenced me with a wave of his hand. "Let me tell the story, will you, Mr. Denson?" he said, his voice rising. He pulled at his nose, apparently reconstructing the scene in his mind before he continued.

"Listen, goddamn it," I said.

But Sir Giles talked right through me. "Then Sheriff Boylan shot her right between the eyes with his pistol. That was what happened to the girl who floated by you on the river and whose memory you cling to with such passionate, ridiculous fervor."

I sat there stunned. What could I say?

Sir Giles pressed on. "It was too late for us to do anything then. We couldn't bring her back to life. As for the Marsdens themselves, we had reason, I suppose, to believe the sheriff would take his wrath out on them." Sir Giles fell silent and tugged at his nose again.

My eyes were glazed, I'm sure. Nick Piper snubbed out

his cigarette in an ashtray and took a sip of martini. Sir Giles's cold-blooded exposition had clearly gotten to him.

"You watched while Boylan murdered Professor Marsden and his wife?"

Sir Giles almost smiled. "I could hardly work up enthusiasm for a dramatic rescue of a man who destroyed both my reputation as a scholar and my chances for a pleasant retirement at Oxford." He paused. "Besides, we were British intelligence officers operating illegally on your soil. With the connivance of the FBI, mind you, but illegally nevertheless."

"Jesus Christ!" said Nick Piper. No one at the table knew Susan Marsden. But Sir Giles's outrageous story hit Nick as hard as it did me. That anyone could be so aloof and callous was vile and outrageous to Nick. He took it personally.

As did I.

"Did the Marsdens tell him what he wanted to know before he murdered them as well?" I asked.

"Oh, yes," said Twigg-Pritchart. "And you may be interested in this." He reached across the table as Carder removed a photograph from his jacket pocket and gave it to him.

Sir Giles gave me the photograph.

It was a picture taken with a telephoto lens, of Boylan dragging the nude body of Susan Marsden by the ankles. Boylan was knee-deep in water. Susan was about to be launched on her way toward the drift at Steamboat. It was the girl in the drift, there was no doubt of that.

For some reason I began to tremble at the sight of the picture. My eyes began to water. I couldn't help it.

"I'm sorry," said Sir Giles. He was a man who had spent the greater part of his life manipulating and sometimes eliminating human life, but even he was moved by the sight of a grown man bawling at the sight of a photograph.

Nick Piper was plain pissed. "Listen here, you son of a

bitch." His small eyes narrowed and I thought he was going to give Sir Giles his best version of a left hook.

"That's okay, Nick," I said. I mopped my eyes with the back of my jacket sleeve. I had to get control of myself because Margo and Helen were beginning to water up as well. The emotion was catching.

"We held on to the photograph because we needed it to blackmail Boylan on the off chance he might recover the manuscript before we did. Besides which, we were in violation of the law in not reporting the murder and what Mr. Carder saw. Her Majesty's Government would not allow a British agent to appear in an American murder trial." Sir Giles kept his eye on Nick Piper. He was apparently concerned that the disheveled professor with the egg yolk on his tie might try to take him on.

"After the murders, you grabbed Boylan, loosened him up with a drug, and found out where Marsden mailed the manuscript?" I was in control of myself again.

"We have a drug superior even to that developed by you Americans. Boylan will remember being surprised by one of my men, but unless the needle bruised his arm, he will have no idea that he was unconscious for twenty minutes. But to answer your question directly, yes, that's what we did." Sir Giles looked amused. "Tell me, Mr. Denson, what do you propose to do now?"

It was a good question. "There is the obvious matter of money. But first, justice in the matter of Susan Marsden's death," I said. "Mr. Boylan is a sheriff overcome by greed. Few will believe he murdered three people in cold blood. Certainly it is asking too much for an officer of the law to be convicted on circumstantial evidence. You have direct evidence."

"Direct evidence, Mr. Denson, which will never be used in a court of law."

"I understand that. You are operating here extralegally

with the implicit cooperation of the FBI. There is no way I can force your hand on the matter of evidence."

"No way," Sir Giles agreed.

"However, you have the power to balance the scales of justice equally as easily as you thwarted them."

He raised an eyebrow.

"You're asking me to save your taxpayers a sum of money?"

"I am that," I said. "Then we'll talk about compensation for our efforts. Only then."

Sir Giles smiled. He took a small leather-bound notebook from his jacket pocket and scribbled a short note. He handed the note to Carder, who read it, crumpled it into an ashtray, and lighted it with a Zippo lighter.

Carder glanced at me and left.

"What will happen, Mr. Denson, is that Sheriff Boylan will be dead in a few minutes. There will be some commotion on the train. The proper medical examiner will examine the body and conclude that he died of a heart attack. It will be obvious and no questions will be asked."

It was not hard for me to smile at the idea of Boylan's getting his. "No way for it to be detected?"

"Absolutely no way under the sun," said Sir Giles.

CHAPTER 15

We fell silent for a few minutes and listened to the *cl-click, cl-click, cl-click.* I thought about trains. I liked trains. I had wanted one when I was a kid, but my parents were not in the electric-train income bracket. If I ever have a son, I'll buy him an electric train so I can play with it.

Philip Boylan, who had no doubt been a decent man for most of his life, had checked into a hotel room at the wrong time and had been overwhelmed by greed.

He had murdered three people.

He was about to die.

We knew that, those of us in the club car. We knew that and we were alone with our thoughts.

Sir Giles seemed unconcerned.

I picked up with the negotiations.

"Now about the financial settlement," I said. "In Duke's yesterday you offered to match the girls' price. That was a hundred fifty thousand dollars. Still a nice figure. The way I see it is that it breaks down to fifty thousand dollars for the real Katheryn Marsden, who has lost both her parents and her sister. Then there is twenty-five thousand dollars each for the girls who took an extra risk in double-crossing you and twenty-five thousand each for Nick and myself who had the foresight not to let you get your hands on everything at once. We're not greedy. I'll see that the real Katheryn Marsden gets her share."

Sir Giles thought about that for a second. "That much and no more. You have your choice of West German deutsche marks or Japanese yen. New bills, small denominations."

Nick Piper was grinning broadly. If he had been enraged by Sir Giles moments earlier, he now admired him in a grudging way. Nick was watching the negotiations as he might a tennis match.

I wasn't really sure whether Margo and Helen were breathing or not. They were so close to the promised land. So close.

I turned to Piper. "Nick, how would you like yours?"

"I'll take the yen," he said. "Easy to peddle in Honolulu."

"You sell mine also?"

"Sure." Piper had himself a slug of martini. This was turning out to be a lot of fun.

"Then it's yen for me," I said. "And how about you girls?"

Sir Giles was amused by it all. It was as though I were a parent asking my kids whether they preferred chocolate, strawberry, butter brickle, or pistachio.

The girls clearly did not know how to answer. The idea of Japanese yen clearly appalled them. It was not romantic. It was shoddy, tacky, like cheap Japanese toys.

"Will the deutsche marks spend in Europe?" asked Helen.

"Certainly," said Sir Giles, playing the role of a well-dressed British Santa Claus. "Phoebe, would you be so kind?"

Phoebe rose to get the money.

"By the way," I said, "will that cute little birthmark wash off?"

"It's gone already," she grinned.

While she was gone the conductor hurried up the aisle toward the front of the train. It was obvious something had gone wrong.

"Poor Mr. Boylan," observed Sir Giles.

"I think I read somewhere that police work is hard on a man's body," I said.

"Very hard, I'm told," said Sir Giles.

"While we're waiting for Phoebe and before we complete our agreement, there are some questions that remain unanswered. Those kinds of questions bother me, as I'm sure they do you."

Sir Giles smiled. "I'll do my best," he said.

"For starters, why did Boylan say the girl was Katheryn Marsden when he knew very well she was Sister Susan?"

"Easy, he wanted to beat me to the mailbox. As chief investigating officer of a murder, he wired the FBI in San Francisco the next morning and asked that a hold be placed on Katheryn Marsden's mail. Not a bad gambit, I would say. He might even have gotten away with it had not Dr. Lindbloom ruined it with his business about four-leaf clovers."

"You found out about the hold request the next morning?"

"The second day, while you were driving your Fiat south."

I filled my plastic cup with beer. That all checked. "But the real action took place a day earlier, when Margo and Helen sat down to drink coffee with their morning paper. They learned just about everything they needed to know, including the value of the package Katheryn had received by Express mail that morning."

Sir Giles gave Helen and Margo a mild look of approbation. "I'm afraid so."

"So that they had the play stashed away in the bus locker by the time you arrived a couple of hours later with a bribe and a small request?"

I wasn't sure, but I thought Carder was trying to restrain a grin.

"Yes, that appears to have been what happened," said Sir Giles. "We were assured by everybody we talked to here that mail service in America is abominable and getting worse. They talked about a man on a horse beating the mail from New York to Washington. We were assured that it would take an absolute minimum of three days for the mail to go from Eugene, Oregon, to Miss Marsden's box in San Francisco. It took one, thanks to your Express mail."

I agreed with Carder. I thought that was funny too. "And since you hadn't time to provide Margo with forged identification, you told her about the birthmark, just in case."

I turned to Helen. "What did you two do after you got rid of the manuscript?"

"We called your answering service in Seattle. You sounded like you were enough of a screwball to help us out. We were wondering how we were going to impersonate Katheryn when Sir Giles showed up with some pocket money and that little tidbit about the birthmark. It was all we needed to con you."

Indeed it was.

Helen had a big grin on her face. "You seemed willing enough. I knew we had it made the way you zeroed in on Margo's butt."

"What the hell?" I said. "Can I help it if Margo has a

good-looking behind? So you called Phoebe in London after you found out about the mail hold, eh, Sir Giles?"

"Yes," he said curtly. Twigg-Pritchart did not like being wrong.

Phoebe returned a few minutes later with two BOAC airline bags. "Deutsche marks for the ladies and yen for the gentlemen," she said. She handed one bag to Nick and the other to Margo.

"I believe we still have some of Sir Giles's property, Nick."

Piper grinned. He leaned over and pulled a manila envelope from under the carpet. He gave it to Sir Giles, who unfastened the metal clasp and examined the contents.

"It's a pleasure doing business with gentlemen," Sir Giles said. "But there's something I don't understand, and I'm like you, I don't like unanswered questions either."

"What's that?" I asked.

"Why were you willing to settle for a hundred fifty thousand dollars? I wouldn't have given you any more and that's the truth. But you didn't know that. The question is, why?"

CHAPTER 16

Why? the man asked. It was a simple question. The smart thing to do would have been to play dumb. A dumb act might cause Sir Giles to pause for a moment. He would wonder if I were perhaps a step ahead of him. But in the end he'd think not; that would not be possible. And what about me? I had my victory assured. What more did I want?

I wanted him to know I had won.

What was victory, after all, if your opponent didn't know he had been beaten. A victory without defeat was no victory at all. That was the bottom line. I could send him a note afterward in care of Her Majesty the Queen and say, "Har, har, har, you stupid bloody Englishman."

But that wouldn't do either. It was a cheap shot. Zane Grey wouldn't approve. Neither did I.

Poking a stick at a Doberman pinscher is generally not my idea of a grand time. But Sir Giles had once killed a man who would have been me had I not been too weak-willed to murder. So I had to take him on. And if I issued him a challenge, I could not choose the weapon as well. An academic squabble over William Shakespeare had brought us here. The challenge had to be literary.

That's what I told myself. Then again, maybe I was just drunk. Maybe I was showing off for Helen or Nick Piper. Who knows? All of the sudden I remembered, just happened to remember, the problem the Virginian had in getting Trampas and a bunch of hell-raising cowboys back to the ranch for roundup. They were on a train, passing through mining country, when Trampas and the boys decided to try for some fast bucks in the mines.

Well now, the Virginian had to buy a little time, had to keep them on the train.

So he told them an outrageous story about money to be made raising frogs in Tumulare County, California.

Yes, sir, he said, the folks in San Francisco just went nuts over frogs' legs. All you had to do was scoop 'em up in a big net now and then; the rest of the time you laid around in the shade and drank beer.

Trampas and the cowpokes went for it. A little western humor there. I decided to steal a bit from Owen Wister. A dumb-ass stunt, I suppose.

"Let's all have a drink," I said. "I have a story to tell. Professor Piper and Professor Twigg-Pritchart are both literary men. Sir Giles, for all his problems with Anston Marsden, has an earned doctorate from Oxford, and the appropriate scholarly publications. His by-line appears regularly in the *Times Literary Supplement*." I winked at Nick. He had his fingers laced together in front of his face. He peered up at me over his knuckles, closed his eyes once and opened them again slowly. Nick was afraid I was about to do something foolish. He was right.

"You wanted to know why, Sir Giles. Tell me, have you ever watched a television program called *The American Sportsman*?"

Sir Giles was feeling good, the bastard. He was willing to murder to get his hands on a missing play by William Shakespeare, a manuscript he intended to destroy in order to spite a dead man. "No, I don't believe I have," he said placidly. He ordered a round for everyone. It was a gesture that had to be seen to be appreciated. Alec Guinness might have pulled it off.

I watched his bland eyes. A gamesman, he fancied himself.

"It's a program about hunting and fishing," I said. "A sportscaster takes a celebrity out to shoot a few birds or catch some fish. Burt Reynolds fishing for tarpon off the Florida Keys. Richard Burton shooting wild turkeys and drinking the same in Arkansas. Norman Mailer shooting pronghorn antelope in Wyoming. George C. Scott fishing for salmon off the mouth of the Columbia. That sort of thing."

"I see," said Sir Giles. I couldn't tell if he did or not. I didn't care. I took another drink paid for by Her Majesty's coin.

"Will this story get us to Portland?" Margo asked.

I pushed my cheek out with my tongue and looked at her out of the corner of my eye. "This story'll get you to the casinos of Monte Carlo if that's *your* druthers."

I couldn't see any more farm lights outside. I knew we were approaching the Siskiyous. We would be in Oregon soon. I could see Twigg-Pritchart was wondering just what this all had to do with my asking for only $150,000.

I figured let him wonder. The conductor had apparently overheard the introduction to my story and was standing at a proper distance, eavesdropping.

"Everybody's welcome here," I said. "This is a story about stomping mice." The conductor grinned and moved closer. Sir Giles didn't appreciate his presence. I didn't give a damn. "The desert of eastern Oregon is a place whose monotony is broken only by the gentle breezes that flow over the land, usually from the west. It's a constant struggle between orifice and sand, and I can tell you a weary sphincter it is that spends its life in that country. The rules of a stomp are simple enough. There is one pickup truck, one nondrinking driver, and maybe a dozen stompers. In order to have it count, a stomper must chug a bottle of beer after he flattens a mouse. The last two stompers to score get the advantage of the running boards. The rest have to crowd onto the truck's bed and suffer that handicap. When the first ruby eyes are spotted, the cry goes up. You must remember your Melville here, Nick."

I stood up and gestured grandly as I imagined Ahab must have when he spotted the mighty whale. Maybe it was Starbuck or Queequeg who spotted it, I don't know. I stood up anyway.

"There goes the little bastard!" I shouted in the direction of the conductor. He fiddled with the bill of his cap, uncertain as to whether he should let this continue.

I had forgotten the rocking motion of the train and almost fell down. I didn't care. I was feeling good. I had just skinned Sir Giles out of $150,000 and I was about to rub it in just to see if he caught on.

"This particular stomp took place on a warm summer night. The stars were out and there was a soft and friendly moon. We were young and in our prime and feeling good. There were plenty of mice and I was ready. I had anticipation. The knack of timing it so that mouse and heel arrived at the same time. It wasn't easy, especially when we were drunk."

Sir Giles raised his hand.

"Sir Giles?"

"Do you still have that touch, Mr. Denson? When you're drunk, I mean." He watched me carefully.

I grinned. "If you think I've had too much to drink, you're right, Sir Giles. But the answer is yes, I still drink and anticipate. I'm a piss artist, as they say in the pubs."

I walked to the far end of the club car and turned to face Sir Giles. I spread my feet slightly and shifted my weight to the balls of my feet. I bent my knees and extended my arms, palms of my hands turned out. "You're a follower of football, Sir Giles. You know a good keeper has to have anticipation. That's the trick. You also know that from the intelligence business. It's much the same with stomping mice. The little bastards will try anything, including reversing their field and scurrying over the top of your foot. You have to have anticipation. Random stomping won't do it."

With that I moved down the carpet of the Amtrak club car, weaving this way and that, stomping imaginary mice as I kept my eye on Sir Giles.

I settled into my seat.

"Are you anticipating me, Mr. Denson?"

I gave him my affable John Denson smile. "I was known for my bravura performances on Epic Mouse Stomps, which are to be distinguished from Casual Mouse Stomps in which no more than three or four mice are ground into the sand on an evening's whim. Not as satisfying as hunting grizzlies in Alaska with Clint Eastwood, but not bad when you're only seventeen years old. An Epic Stomp is high adventure. Those who can't hit a mouse may drink or not as they see fit; mostly they drink. Vomiting is entirely in order. I was best in the final hours of the stomp when the dizzies begin to overwhelm the participants."

"No modesty there," said Helen.

I had never seen such gorgeous eyes on a human. I wanted to hustle her back to the sleeping car right then and there but I couldn't. In addition to the fact that she probably wouldn't go anyway; my usefulness was over. Almost.

"We have to remember that this is a parable of sorts, for Sir Giles's benefit," I said. "In the course of that extraordinary night, I had stomped eight mice, beating the storied record by two. About half of the stompers had dropped out of the action and were wallowing miserably in assorted fluids that had collected in the back of the truck. It was an awful mess. I had the right-hand board. The halfback son of an electrical engineer was on the left board. He earned that spot the second mouse out and had regained it repeatedly on his way to seven mice. It was time to quit. Several stompers were sick and I could have had the record had I agreed. It was a simple thing.

"But I said no. I wanted to push on for the impossible ten mice."

Sir Giles interrupted. "The one point five million."

I looked at him. "Think of it. The greatest mouse stomper of all time. Just two more mice. But my pals weren't going to let me have the record without a fight. They had pride, I'll grant them that. They sucked in deep gulps of clean night air in an effort to dispel the dizzies. The driver called out of the window that he was heading for Longnekker's Hump and everybody leaned forward just a little."

I paused for a drink. I had a bit of a buzz on. So did Nick Piper. He was a fine man; I could see it in his eyes. Neither of us was being too smart.

"Longnekker's Hump was an abrupt U-shaped rise in the desert, several hundred yards across the mouth. For some unexplained reason there were more mice inside the hump than anywhere else in the desert. All Epic Stomps eventually wound up inside Longnekker's Hump.

"The last mouse had been a good one. It didn't cower in front of the headlights, and I had covered fifty yards on a full bladder, reversing my field several times and falling down twice, before I drilled it into the sand with my heel. It was a brave mouse. I thought about Hemingway. I reflected on what being a man was all about." I grinned at Nick and he was laughing. Sir Giles knew I was trying to pull something on him. He didn't think it was funny.

"About a hundred yards from the mouth of the hump, I urinated into an empty beer bottle. And as we entered the marvelous interior of Longnekker's Hump I flipped some urine into the wind, just above the cab of the truck. It was a perfect shot. The wind caught the piss and whipped it through the darkness, square into the faces of my competitors. They had no warning at all. Sir Giles, why do you suppose I did that? I had already won the stomp that night. I had set records in the process. And I had no real competition for that last mouse. The halfback on the left board was drunk."

"I'm hardly intoxicated, Mr. Denson."

"Your case is similar, but different, Sir Giles."

"How is that?"

I was thinking of arrogance, but I ignored him. "The driver, thinking the protests were a call for more speed, goosed the ancient engine whose connecting rods were already thumping loudly. The pickup lurched forward, hurtling over stunted cactus and sandy bumps as it penetrated the interior of Longnekker's Hump. Every time a weary face appeared above the cab, I knocked it down with a flick of my wrist. I had plenty of urine in reserve. The problem was that those in the back of the truck now wanted that mouse more than ever. This last part is hard to tell. I think we need another round of drinks."

Sir Giles did the honors.

I continued. "We were well into the interior of the hump before we realized it and the driver, who must have been confused, headed directly for the rim itself. That was rarely done. The truck hurtled over so fast that all four wheels left the desert. When it crunched down on compressed springs, the driver saw what he thought was a mouse skitter to the left. Later, some claimed it was a McDonald's French fry bag strayed miles from civilization. We never knew for sure.

"Anyway, the driver turned sharply in the direction of the movement and gunned the motor. He rammed an enormous sagebrush and the engine conked out. The truck was facing the wind. Here it was that I forgot everything I had learned about knowing your limits, about moderation, about control, about when to take a chance and when not to. I also forgot about the wind."

"What did you do?" Helen asked.

"I emptied my bottle square into the wind so that I might have an unimpeded go at that last mouse."

"And then?"

"I caught it square in the face. I lost my balance and pitched forward, bouncing off the fender before I hit the ground. The universe was a pale gray with tiny spots. And then I saw not one, not two, but three sets of ruby spots. Those were frightened eyes, friends, pinned by the headlights of the truck. One by one they disappeared under the heel of the halfback son of the electrical engineer.

"And that's why, Sir Giles, I tagged you for only a hundred fifty thousand."

I looked at Nick Piper. He winced.

Sir Giles took a measured sip of Scotch.

"There are several ways of looking at it," I said. "There is the matter of knowing your limits. That's important. My father's advice never to eat yellow snow does not apply. But his advice to never, but never, piss into the wind, I suppose does."

"An amusing story, Mr. Denson, but I'm not sure what it proves," said Sir Giles. He did not smile.

"Not as classy as flushing grouse in Scotland. Good dogs, twenty-caliber Brownings, gamekeepers and all that."

"I think I should give your story a little thought." Sir Giles rose. "I'll be turning in now, Mr. Denson, Professor Piper." He shook our hands and disappeared in the direction of the sleeping car.

Carder followed his superior. Before he left the club car, he turned and looked back to our table. He shook his head, grinned, and disappeared.

CHAPTER 17

The train began to slow for the ascent of the Siskiyou Mountains.

Nick Piper stood up and held onto the table for support. "I'm not certain you should have done that, John."

I wasn't sure the girls understood what he meant.

"What do you mean?" asked Margo.

Nick gestured for me to answer.

"What he means is that I'm too damned clever for my own good. Sir Giles is having second thoughts about our bargain. If he thinks the manuscript is phony, he'll try to get his money back. But with him it's not the money that counts. Her Majesty's Government budgets that for overseas operations. It's his ego that matters most. I challenged him, and Sir Giles is not a man to back down from a challenge."

"For God's sake, Gary Cooper at high noon! Why in the hell did you do that?" To say that Helen was pissed is to put it mildly.

I shrugged my shoulders stupidly. "For the dumbest of all reasons, I suppose. Pride. I also wanted to stick it to the son of a bitch. There was always a chance the truth wouldn't come to him until later, after he'd been had. But now I'm not so sure. I think what I may have to do in a few minutes, friends, is jump off this train with two BOAC bags full of currency . . ."

"The little dance you mentioned," said Piper.

"Just two steps, a tuck, and a little luck."

"Wait a minute," Helen interrupted.

"One goddamn minute," said Margo. She gripped the table so hard her knuckles turned white.

"Let me finish. This is important. If for any reason I have to jump, the three of you get off the train at Eugene and find a hotel or motel somewhere. Tomorrow call my answering service in Seattle. You call, Nick. Identify yourself as Natty Bumppo and say, 'Yond Denson has a lean and hungry look;/He thinks too much: such men are dangerous!' "

Piper laughed.

"Can you remember that?"

"Cooper and Shakespeare, how can I forget?" he grinned.

"Good. Because if you don't give me that line, Emma won't tell you where to meet me. And ladies, if you are thinking of playing fun games, my gal Emma will have a question for the caller that no one except Nick will be able to answer."

Helen closed her eyes and took a deep breath. "I think we've learned our lesson about double-crossing people. But what I want to know is, will Sir Giles keep after us until he gets his money back?"

"No," I lied. The truth was Sir Giles would have his revenge. But I was responsible, not the girls, not Nick Piper. It was my hide on the line, not theirs. After his cold-blooded description of what happened to the Marsden family, I didn't much give a damn. The girls and Nick didn't need to know that. "The code business is just a precaution. I think if

I make it off the train tonight, he'll let it drop. London gave him permission for this caper as a favor. He has his limits. He's been beaten before. He's not infallible. He might make a token effort tomorrow, but not much more."

Carder appeared in the doorway.

"Mr. Denson, Sir Giles asks that you remain in the club car for a few minutes. He'd like to continue our chat."

"Figures," I said. I picked up the two bags of money.

Carder drew a small pistol from his pocket. Wicked-looking thing. He no doubt knew how to use it. It was night outside. Truth and points north were coming up. There were just the two girls, Piper, myself, and Carder in the club car. There was the bartender too, but he was rattling bottles in a storeroom barely larger than a closet.

My underwear had been riding up all evening. I stood up and pulled at my pants.

Nick Piper cleared his throat.

The girls didn't say anything.

I scratched the top of my head. A bewildered hayseed gesture. I needed time to think. I considered scratching my behind, but thought better of it. Enough was enough. "You know," I said, "they tried to teach me how to shoot those little things. Never could get the hang of it. Had cardboard people popping out of the ground and all that. Didn't make any difference. My instructors enjoyed having me around, like a lovable dog, so they faked my scores."

"I can believe that," said Carder. "Is that why you botched the job on Duncan McDonald? Did you just miss?"

"No, I could have pranged him. But he had a wife and two kids. What good would it have done? You have to consider ends and means. I'll bet you've pranged people before, for the good of Queen and Country. Am I being too philosophical for you?"

We listened to the *click, cl-click, cl-click* of steel on steel. Carder said nothing.

"I know, sometimes consequences dictate. You're representing the British people, after all. Who were you representing when you stood there and watched Boylan murder a professor, his wife, and his daughter?"

Carder didn't blink, not once.

"Did you represent the British people then? Suppose the manuscript had been real? The best service to the British people then would have been to get it to the British Museum. Sir Giles wouldn't have done that. He would have burned it to prove a point. You know that and I know it. What did he say to you when you returned to your sleeping coach?"

Carder smiled. "He wanted to know what I thought of your curious little story."

"Let me guess, you told him it was bloody nonsense."

He laughed this time. He lowered the pistol to the side of his leg so the bartender couldn't see it should he emerge from the storeroom. "Something like that," he said.

I ran my tongue over my front teeth. I could have used a toothbrush. "What about the anticipation part and the know-your-limits stuff? I thought that was pretty good."

Carder shook his head. "The only reason you wouldn't ask for the maximum was if the manuscript was a fake. If you had asked for a half-million dollars, say, Sir Giles would have had the play examined in a laboratory. British security is not at stake here and we do have limits. But one hundred fifty thousand dollars. We could swing that."

"Sir Giles examined the play at his leisure," I said. "It's real."

"It may not be, Mr. Denson. Just sit tight, please; I have my instructions." A man entered the club car on his way to the sleeping coach. Carder took a seat and hid the pistol under his jacket.

I waited for the man to pass. "When would I have had time to check it out?"

Carder grinned. "Funny, that's exactly the same question Sir Giles asked."

"You told him about the envelope with the blank paper inside?"

"It was a strange little dash your lady friend made at the lockers. I've been thinking about it all day."

"And your conclusion?"

"You needed a diversion to stash a couple of sheets for Professor Piper to examine at something more than mere leisure."

"I did it with a magnet on top of the locker. You glanced at the bottom, which was empty enough."

"How did you expect to get the manuscript off the train had it been real?"

I laughed. "Jump, what else? You'll notice the train has slowed considerably the last few minutes. We're ascending a pass over the Siskiyou Mountains."

Helen interrupted. She looked like she was ready to cry. "Then why didn't you jump? Why did you wait?"

I looked at her like she was a trifle touched. "Why, that's dangerous as hell. I could break an ankle, a leg, or my damned fool neck. Mr. Carder, would you tell the ladies and Professor Piper here the first rule of planning an operation, even so simple a one as my getting off this train?"

"Backups."

"Backups?" asked Piper.

"A primary plan and an alternate," I said. "Something can always go wrong. If you don't have a backup, you can get screwed."

"What Mr. Denson is saying is that he was willing to take a chance that Sir Giles would not ask the questions he did until later. Mr. Denson lost. Now that I'm here, he has to go to his second choice. I'm curious as to what that is."

"So am I," said Nick.

It was clear from the looks on the girls' faces that they were curious also.

I snapped my fingers. "Well, hell, Andrew. What do you say you do me a favor? The security of Her Majesty's Government is not at stake here, only Sir Giles's ego. The money's small potatoes."

Carder pulled at his earlobe with his free hand. It would have to be I who made the pitch, not he.

"Okay, what I'm asking is that you tell Sir Giles I had already jumped by the time you got here."

I could feel my heart beating. I wished I had clean socks.

Carder thought it over for a minute that seemed like a month. He cleared his throat, looked at Piper, then at me again.

"One hell of a story for back home," I said.

"Is my dislike of Sir Giles that obvious?"

"To me, it is. I don't think Sir Giles notices. He's too much in love with himself to see people hate his guts."

"This would have to be among friends," he said.

"No reason for it to be otherwise."

Carder looked at Piper and the girls.

"Oh, of course," said Nick. The girls nodded yes.

Carder put away his pistol and bowed to Helen and Margo. "I congratulate you on your choice of Mr. Denson, ladies. Have a nice ride now."

He grinned at me, turned, and disappeared in the direction of Sir Giles's sleeper.

When the door closed after him, I mopped my forehead with the back of my hand, which was trembling visibly. "I think maybe there was one part of my story Sir Giles might have paid more attention to."

"Anticipation?" asked Piper.

"That's it," I closed my eyes and took a deep breath. It was hard to stop shaking.

Helen looked exhausted. "I don't understand."

"Carder can't stand Twigg-Pritchart. I've known that since yesterday. I imagine there are a lot of British agents around the world who feel that way. This was a perfect chance for them to get even without hurting their government. Sir Giles overlooked that possibility. I thought he might."

Helen came up and gave me a kiss. "You take it easy now, Stomping John. I don't want you to get hurt."

I could hardly believe it. Me, John Denson. I felt like Cary Grant. Or maybe the young man who gets kissed goodbye by Maureen O'Hara before he goes off to die with the boys on Omaha Beach. Maureen doesn't know he's going to die, but everybody else does.

I swallowed. I wanted to take her in my arms and really plant one on her. Cary could pull that off, but I'd blow it. She would probably have said the same thing if I had an enormous, unsqueezed pimple in the middle of my forehead.

Besides that, she had twenty-five grand riding on me.

"I'll do my damnedest," I said. I grabbed her for one more quick kiss. It seemed genuine enough. I decided to let well enough alone.

I turned and walked to the exit in the front of the car and, without pausing or looking back, opened the door. The train was going as slow as it ever would.

The mountain air was as cold as a well-digger's ass.

Now there are bad ways and better ways of jumping off a moving train. There are no good ways. The bad way is to leap off like a paratrooper over Normandy, hoping to land on both feet at once. Do that and you'll wind up tumbling end over end like a tenpin. I know that from experience.

The better way is to hold onto the train with your right hand and extend your left foot as far and as low as you can.

The theory is that you land on your left foot and use your second step to control your tumble.

Those first two steps are neither easy nor elegant.

I sucked in a lungful of cold air to counter the alcohol. I needed to let my eyes get adjusted to the darkness. I waited for the shadows to become trees and rocks. The gentle *click, cl-click, cl-click* inside the car became an ear-shattering *boom, clacka, boom, clacka, boom, clacka, boom.* I doubled my right leg underneath me and took a firm grip on the doorjamb as low as I could manage.

And I stretched. The Lady was out there waiting. Time to flash my style.

The *boom, clacka, boom* thundered even louder.

I dropped the money with my left hand. I tried to get a fix on the railroad bed, but it was a blur. My right hand began to slip. I let go and pushed hard with my leg.

Rudolf Nureyev might have pulled it off.

I had a little trouble.

I landed on my left foot. My knee buckled, which I expected. My ankle fractured, which I hadn't. I had two problems: The train was going faster than I thought and the grade was flanked by a steep downhill bank.

My right foot didn't make it on its turn, and I wasn't able to control my roll. My left collarbone popped.

The bank was steep. What happened was simple: I tumbled wildly into the night.

The only thing that slowed me was a fir tree near the bottom of the bank.

Virgin timber. Bigger than I was by a damned sight.

The Siskiyou Two-Step. Claiborne's dance. One hell of a turn around the floor. Anyone with half a brain would pass. Maybe stay home and watch television. Maybe bullshit with the boys. Dream other dreams. But not me. I won't do that. I'll step right out there and take on the Lady. Take Her in my arms. Hold Her close. Breast against chest. Rib on rib.

Thigh against thigh. Smell Her hair and feel Her breathe. Once you've done that and survived, you look at life a little differently. You're not as hard on people.

For me small things matter more: a hunk of cauliflower, a little wine, maybe a joint now and then, a laugh here and there, kissing a girl on the neck and telling her she's lovely. That kind of thing.

I tasted salt. Blood. I was dizzy. It occurred to me for no reason that the FBI man, Richard Montgomery, knew Margo wasn't Katheryn. Since I didn't ask him, he didn't tell me. Probably thought it was funny. A man with a sense of humor.

The train had long since gone by the time my head cleared. I decided to wait it out at the bottom of the grade. The cold air sobered me. My ankle began to swell. My arm was paralyzed with pain. I began to sweat. Then shake. My jaw chattered in great, spastic, shuddering runs. The damned thing wouldn't stop. I thought I was going to lose the enamel on my teeth. I watched the Big Dipper and waited. When it got light, I would make myself a crutch and retrieve the money.

By the time the glow appeared in the east, my ankle was as thick as a stump. My shoulder was white with pain. But I did it. I ripped a branch off a dead pine with my good arm and made a crutch of sorts. I couldn't use it on the way up the grade. I had to push it in front of me while I inched upward on my stomach like some great, sweating, tortured worm. My eyes were blinded by pain. It must have been about eleven o'clock when I made it to the top; the trees in the forest were beginning to make a popping sound from the heat. I stood up and the knee of my good leg buckled from fatigue. I got up again. I wish Zane Grey could have seen me. The pain was so bad nothing else mattered.

Well, maybe honor did. And simple justice. Words abused by unthinking, uncivilized bastards.

The airline bags were there, waiting. I slung them over

my right shoulder and began the long hobble that had all the prospects of a death march. It would take me all day to reach the bottom of the other side. By then I would be in Oregon. As a matter of fact, I wouldn't be far from Ashland, the home of a summertime Shakespearean festival said to be one of the two or three best in Canada and the United States. I wondered if they had a good hospital.

The girl on the North Umpqua was the last thing on my mind during that walk. I thought instead of Helen and those marvelous hazel eyes. Maybe there was some chemistry there after all. Just maybe. If there was, I would set a Guinness record for holding tight the longest. Boy, did I need it!

It didn't hurt to think about Sir Giles Twigg-Pritchart either. He would be on that train livid with rage at being skinned out of a hundred fifty grand by a dart-throwing flake. I was glad I let him know. As the British would say, it bloody well served him right for instructing his agents to do nothing while Philip Boylan murdered three people in cold blood. Three people!

I took on the rest of the Siskiyou grade one outrageous railroad tie at a time. The trick was not to think about the pain. Marathon runners learned that long ago. If you think about the hurt, it'll tear you apart. If I thought about the pain, I wouldn't make it. But what could I think about that would make me forget? What really mattered that much? Creation? The primordial ooze? Black holes way out in the universe? No. Were there people who made a difference? Sally Rand, the fan dancer? Einstein? Eisenhower? No. Beethoven? Bobby Kennedy? No. Christ, I was hallucinating. What mattered?

Me. I mattered. Human beings mattered. My ankle throbbed wildly, but I kept moving.

I thought again. What else mattered? What else could help?

Someone once told me the motto of the Texas Rangers. That was it. The motto of the Texas Rangers: Little man whip a big man every time if the little man's in the right and just keeps coming. Wasn't that nice? Wasn't it sweet? Wouldn't it be lovely? Maybe that's why my old pal Zane Grey was so popular. That's the way things worked out in his books.

That's why I was a private detective.

I remembered another one. The epitaph of a cowboy buried in Tombstone: HE DONE HIS DAMNEDEST.

What would my epitaph say?

HERE LIES JOHN DENSON, ROMANTIC, CYNIC, DREAMER, FOOL. HE TRIED, GOD KNOWS. HE CARED ABOUT THE TRUTH.

A slight breeze stirred midmorning. It felt cool against my shirt. The wind made a melancholy, lowing sound in the tops of the evergreens. The sky was deep blue. The air was clear and smelled of pine. The nights were cold in the Siskiyous, but the days were hot this time of year. As the sun rose higher, grasshoppers began to stir about the railroad right-of-way. I heard a meadowlark in the distance. I saw a hawk riding the updrafts. This was the splendid wilderness men in cities dream of—or say they do anyway. One night in a sleeping bag with sand in it usually changes their minds.

It was a wilderness that stood a chance of getting the best of me if I let it. The crutch wasn't much good for taking the weight off my fractured ankle because that side was where my collarbone had popped. So mostly I hopped on my right leg, which was weak and getting weaker. I had to make it out that day. I couldn't risk the shock on my system of spending another cold night in the mountains.

It was close to high noon when I spotted the trestle across the Klamath River. The river began at the Klamath basin, the famous resting place for tens of thousands of waterfowl on their way south in the winter. It crossed the California border northwest of Yreka and joined the Trinity River before it emptied into the Pacific just south of Crescent City.

I knew I was in no shape to try for a drink of water from the river, so I struggled on across the trestle. I was about halfway across when I heard it: a faint *whop, whop, whop* in the distance. This wasn't help. No way. I knew in an instant that it was Sir Giles Twigg-Pritchart. I lay down on the trestle, hoping I wouldn't be spotted. The helicopter was flying low over the railroad bed from the top of the grade I had just come down.

It hovered above me for a moment and continued on its way to the end of the trestle. I got to my feet as it settled on the railroad tracks. I was unarmed. I couldn't run. I couldn't jump. Sir Giles let the *whop, whop* cease and the dust settle before he got out. He was in no hurry. He had no doubt spotted my blood back up the line and knew I was badly hurt. A coup de grace was all that was needed.

He walked alone down the center of the track. He was impeccably dressed in a pin-striped, three-piece suit and wore a proper hat. He looked elegant, civilized.

I waited for him, filthy with blood, sweat, and dust. There was just me and fear, nothing else. Gary Cooper at least had his intended hiding in a building, trying to decide whether or not to help him out with a great big old Winchester.

I had no one.

Sir Giles took the precaution of stopping about fifteen feet in front of me. There was no way I could rush him, even with a good ankle. "Well, I must say, Mr. Denson, the scenery out west is indeed everything they say."

"Yes, it's lovely," I said. I used the present tense. I could just as well have put it in the past for all the hope I had of making it off the trestle.

"It looks like you've had a hard day, what with the blood and the dirt and all. I'm impressed, by the way. It's remarkable that you survived the leap off the train, much less have made it this far in your condition. Is your ankle fractured?"

"That and my collarbone. You want your money back?"

"I want my money and your life, Mr. Denson. You tried to cheat me."

He pulled a pearl-handled automatic from his jacket pocket. There was no sense standing there bullshitting with him. The Klamath River was my only chance. I dove for it.

Sir Giles fired the automatic.

My broken ankle slipped between two railroad ties. I went down with a white-hot pain just below the ribs on my left side. I struggled for the edge and the river, but my foot was stuck.

Sir Giles squatted at a safe distance with his pistol in his hand and regarded me with something approaching admiration. "Well done; that's exactly what I would have done in your place. Do you think you could have survived the river?"

I lay there and looked up at him. I couldn't do anything else. "With my ankle and my collarbone maybe. Now I'm not sure." I felt my left side with my right hand. My hand came back wet with blood.

"A nasty wound," said Sir Giles.

"What's next? You leave me here to bleed to death, is that the action?"

Sir Giles looked back at the helicopter. I could see Andrew Carder leaning against it, waiting. "Well, I could do that. I could blow your head off. Or I could push you in the river. Any one of the three would do the job."

"Maybe you could do all three and make sure I was dead, like Rasputin."

"I won't leave you here to bleed to death because you

just might make it to help. You've shown yourself to have extraordinary tenacity. Shooting you in the head is vulgar, fit for Latin Americans perhaps, but not a British intelligence officer. The river is the proper way. Your participation in this affair began with a body in a river; what better way for it to end than the same way?"

I couldn't help but grin at that. "Gives it a certain wholeness."

"Exactly. That appeals to me." Sir Giles removed the two airline bags of money from my right arm. I was almost paralyzed with pain and couldn't move. He placed the bags between the rails and looked at them with distaste. "You've gotten blood all over them," he said.

"I guess it's out darts for me."

Sir Giles smiled. He removed a handkerchief from his pocket and wrapped it around my ankle so he wouldn't get blood on his hands, then jerked my foot free from between the ties. I damned near passed out from the pain. His handkerchief had small black initials in the corner: GTP. He dropped it over the side of the trestle.

I could hear the Klamath River below. It was maybe sixty feet down and there was a current.

Next Sir Giles put his expensive oxfords against a spot on my chest that was merely sweaty, not bloody, and began to push. They were elegant shoes. Lovely things, soft leather.

I helped him out.

(Little man whip a big man every time.)

I rolled.

(If the little man's in the right.)

Grabbed his foot and yanked. Hard. Gritted my teeth.

(And just keeps coming.)

We both plunged off the bridge.

I caught a glimpse of Sir Giles's face as we went over. He looked concerned. I didn't blame him.

The water felt like concrete; thank God I landed on my

right side. I went down, down, holding my breath, then up, up again, stroking for all I was worth with my right arm. When I got to the top, I rolled onto my back and floated for several minutes. I was alive. I wondered if Sir Giles could swim.

Suddenly a hand grabbed me by the collar. A man wearing a blue baseball cap looked down at me. I heard a boy's voice: "Is he alive, Dad?"

"He's alive all right, but he's bleeding like a stuck pig. Clear a spot for him there. You stay on that side of the boat while I pull him in. We don't want to tip her over."

While the boy readied the boat, I considered the bullet wound in my side. The hospital would report it to the police. The police would want to know how it got there. I slipped my good hand into my hip pocket and donated my wallet to the cold waters of the Klamath.

"We're ready if you are," said the man in the baseball cap. He steadied his grip on my collar and grabbed me by the belt.

He heaved me out of the water, almost swamping the boat in the process. I found myself in the bottom of a wooden drift boat.

The boy, who also wore a blue baseball cap, stared at me with his mouth open.

The man shifted his weight in the boat. "We're only about six or eight miles from Yreka. If you've got enough blood, you're gonna be okay," he said.

"Name's John Denson."

"Pleased to meet you, Mr. Denson. I'm Al McKay. This here's my boy, Ted; he's thirteen. We were doing a little drift fishing when Ted spotted you in the water there."

Ted looked like he was going to throw up. "Don't you fret about me, Ted, I'm gonna be okay," I said. I closed my eyes and waited for the current and Al McKay's drift boat to get me to a hospital. The Lady must have been surprised that

I came back for another dance. Twice in one day, and I survived them both.

I remember being bumped around a lot, voices and men carrying me up a steep bank from the river. I remember waiting. I remember being dizzy. I remember hearing another meadowlark while I waited. I remember the ambulance.

I don't remember anything after that.

When I woke up I was between clean sheets. My left foot and ankle were encased in plaster. My left arm and shoulder were held rigid by another cast. The dressing on the bullet wound wasn't quite as bulky. My good arm was being fed fluid through a clear plastic tube.

The girl on the North Umpqua was standing by my bed, watching me.

"That's okay, Mr. Denson. No need to look so startled. I'm Susan's sister, Katheryn."

"You look exactly like her."

"I know. I also know about your meeting her on the North Umpqua and all that followed. Professor Piper told me everything. I flew here from Tokyo yesterday after I learned of my parents' deaths."

"I tried to get something in the way of compensation for you, no matter how inadequate, but it didn't work out."

"Yes, it did." I had been so shocked by the woman standing by my bed that I hadn't seen Nick Piper, who was also in the room. As were Margo and Helen.

I gave Helen a wink and she gave me a weak smile back. Something was wrong there. "How do you figure?" I asked Nick.

"The two airline bags were delivered anonymously to the hospital in your name. The money's all there, plus the original of *Jonathan Claiborne.*"

"Was there a note in either bag?"

Nick held up a slip of white paper. I could see several

hand-lettered words written on it in all caps. "It says, ONLY ONE FISH SWAM," said Nick.

Sir Giles Twigg-Pritchart had drowned in the Klamath River. "Oh," I said.

"Code of some kind, John?"

"I don't have any idea."

Nick looked surprised.

"Well, I'll tell you about it when I'm feeling better," I said. I noticed Margo and Helen were looking anxious. "I suppose you two would like your cut."

They both grinned broadly.

"Which bag's theirs, Nick?"

Nick picked up a BOAC bag. "This one," he said.

"They earned it, I guess."

He barely got it off the floor before Margo had it in her hand.

Both Margo and Helen looked at me uncomfortably. They were embarrassed. There was an awkward silence.

Margo finally spoke. "I think Helen and I better be going for now. Give you and Nick a chance to talk."

Why in the hell would I want to talk to Nick? "Sure," I said.

Helen came up and gave my hand a squeeze. "So long, John."

"Don't ever be ashamed of being from Yakima," I said. "After all, that's how Yakima Canutt got his name." She didn't know about William O. Douglas. She didn't know about Yakima Canutt either.

"Who was he?"

"One of Hollywood's most famous second-unit directors. He was in charge of battle spectacles in epic movies, *Lawrence of Arabia,* that kind of thing."

"Yakima Canutt, I'll remember." Helen paused. It wasn't in her to leave without a word. "I want you to know this business with you wasn't my idea, John. Margo knew you would fall the way you watched me dance that night. She said I had to do it. She said it was the only way to guarantee you wouldn't double-cross us. If it seemed genuine to you, that's because it was a little bit."

Margo avoided my eyes.

I was right about their characters. I had seen it in the way they danced. We all want to be loved. From the beginning, their try for the jackpot had been ingenious. It had also been a gamble. I understood Margo's logic; the opportunity for my seduction was something they couldn't pass up. She knew intuitively what had to be done.

But it was Helen, vulnerable, wounded, used Helen, who had had to see it through. She had turned in a hell of a performance, from that first night in their apartment to the moment I jumped off the train.

"Ah, well," I said.

Margo gave Helen a nudge and they were gone. Helen looked back once. She wasn't a bad person.

"She won't be back, Nick."

"No, I don't imagine so."

I said, "Sucker John."

"She can't wait to spend that twenty-five thousand." Nick wanted to change the subject. "Say, exactly how was it you wound up in the Klamath River anyway?"

I looked at Katheryn Marsden. "The police are going to be calling shortly. What happened was I got robbed on the Amtrak liner north. Guy shot me, took my wallet, and pushed me off the train. I made it as far as the railroad trestle when I passed out and fell into the Klamath River."

"Must have been some fall," Nick said.

"It was a dandy, Nick. Everybody got that straight? That's what happened, nothing more." I looked at Katheryn, then at Nick. They had it square. "Ms. Marsden, I have a personal question to ask you. It's about your . . ."

"My rump. You want to know if I have a birthmark."

I nodded.

"Yes, I do. I've known about it for years."

"After all my trouble, I don't imagine I'll get a chance to see the real McCoy."

Katheryn smiled but didn't say anything. Her smile was marvelous. It was charming, proper, but more than a little suggestive. "If it's okay with you, I'd like to come back in a few days—after I get my family buried. I thought maybe we could talk about your finding Susan in the river and everything that happened after that. The doctor said you'll be here for a couple of months at least. I don't have anything to do. My doctoral dissertation is finished at Berkeley and I can't do anything until I get my committee together."

That's right, she was a schoolmarm. I'd forgotten. Did you hear that, Zane Grey?

"You'll probably get to talk to her all summer, but I get to take her out to dinner tonight," Nick said. He'd had himself an adventure and had more than held up his end of the bargain. Not bad for an old professor.

"You know," I said, "it's remarkable how much you look like your sister." That was true. I'd never seen anything like it.

Katheryn smiled. "I'm three years older than Susan, but everybody said we looked like twins."

Twins was the only word for it. They looked so much alike it was startling.

Just then a nurse came in and said I needed to rest; the police wanted to ask some questions about how I came to have a bullet in me. The schoolmarm leaned over and gave me a soft kiss full on the mouth. I felt like leaping out of bed and pursuing her, casts flapping like hard-leather chaps.

Nick Piper was the last one out of the door. It closed, then reopened. He gave me a big grin and a thumbs-up sign for a job well done. The truth was enough for me. Meeting someone like Nick Piper along the way was just a little extra.